C000051991

# Runnin

## BARRY KAUFMANN-WRIGHT

UPFRONT PUBLISHING
CAMBRIDGESHIRE

RUNNING WILD
Copyright © Barry Kaufmann-Wright 2005

ISBN 978-184426-339-4

First Published 2005 by
UPFRONT PUBLISHING LTD
Cambridgeshire

Also by the author Barry Kaufmann-Wright,
and published by Upfront Publishing:

THE WILDLIFE MAN
(2002)

Printed by Copytech UK Ltd

Also available from the same author

# JACK OF ALL TRADES

The contents of this book are a few amusing incidents that
happened to the author during his time as a rural 'Bobby'
and Wildlife Crime Officer with Essex Police with
whom he served for 32 years.
During his service many varied incidents, both sad and
amusing, occurred which emphasises how a policeman
really is a 'Jack of All Trades'.

Published by Upfront Publishing, 2008
ISBN 978-184426-538-1

Also available from the same author

# THE WILDLIFE MAN

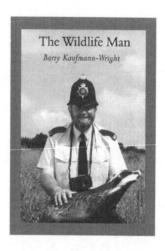

From a very young age, 'The Wildlife Man' loved and
held a fascination with animals.
This is the story of how his passion for wildlife, originally
a hobby, became first a part of his job as a police officer,
then his full-time occupation and his life.
He is respected and admired for his work to this day. This
is a heartfelt book, and the author's passion and appreciation
for wildlife and nature is infectious.

Published by Upfront Publishing, 2002
ISBN 978-184426-026-3

Also available from the same author

# CASSIE

This is an amusing story told by Cassie of her many
adventures and experiences during her very active life,
including assisting her Master in his role as
a Village Bobby.

Published by Upfront Publishing, 2006
ISBN 978-184426-395-0

Also available from the same author

# CHOCKA'S STORY

This is a story of a Labrador called Chocka who
was a stray for sometime before coming to live with
the author and his wife.

Chocka describes her relationship and adventures with her
lifelong pal Chaz and Chaz's pup Chip and the many friends
that she made through her life and of course Barry and Pat.

Published by Upfront Publishing, 2010
ISBN 978-184426-827-6

*All the photographs in this book
are the work of the author.*

# *Acknowledgements*

My wife Pat for her support and patience during the writing of this book.

My colleagues Niki O'Mahony and Dave Smith, my daughter Georgina, and Pat for all their artistry.

Julia Smith who made sense of my 'scribblings'.

Peter Gardner, my father-in-law, for his support.

Gerald Durrell for encouraging me to re-write this story after he read the initial manuscript at Jersey Zoo in 1967.

Finally my grandparents Tom and Freda Wright who owned the farm and who made this story possible.

By Barry Kaufmann-Wright

*This book is dedicated to Judy Rees*

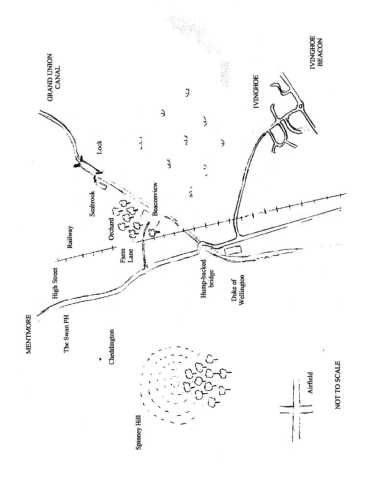

MENTMORE

GRAND UNION CANAL

The Swan PH

High Street

Railway

Lock

Seabrook

Orchard

Beaconview

Cheddington

Farm
Lane

IVINGHOE

Spinney Hill

Hump-backed
bridge

Duke of
Wellington

IVINGHOE
BEACON

Airfield

NOT TO SCALE

*'Seabrook' Canal and Lock*

# Running Wild

This is a story set in 1952 about a fox that lived on the author's farm in the Chilterns in Buckinghamshire. The farm was known as 'Beaconview' and was between the villages of Cheddington and Ivinghoe with Ivinghoe Beacon (a large hill forming part of the Chiltern range) lying to the east of the farm, and another hill to the west. This is called 'Spinney Hill' in the story and there is a small spinney along its eastern flank. The Grand Union Canal and the London Midland Scottish Railway Line ran through the farm. Many of the adventures that happen to the fox are based on real life incidents that happened at that time.

## Some hunting terms and their meanings

**The Hunt Master** is the huntsman or woman in charge of the hunt.

**The Whipper in** is the huntsman in charge of the hounds.

**The Field** are the horses and riders which hunt that day.

**The Meet** is where the hunt gathers before riding off.

**The Terrier Man** is the person in charge of the terriers used for flushing the fox if it disappears into a pipe or hole.

**The Followers** are the people who are not members of the hunt but who will attend the meet and follow the hunt either on foot or by various methods of transport.

**'Charlie'** is the fox.

**'Charlie's away'** is the call used by the huntsmen or the followers if the fox breaks cover and runs.

**Gone to earth** or **gone to ground** is the term used if the fox disappears into a hole or pipe.

These are but a few of the many hunting terms and phrases.

# Chapter One
# THE YOUNG FOX

It was a cold February morning and the foxhounds were in full cry after the vixen. The low sun that hung over the hills to the east sparkled in the frost-laden undergrowth. The hounds had picked up the scent of the vixen at Mentmore Park where she had rested up after a night's hunting. Her earth was in the railway embankment some way off near the canal.

The vixen was running along the bottom of the embankment having crossed the line twice in her attempts to lose the hunt. She was now returning to the safety of her earth but the hounds were rapidly closing in on her. Her pace was slowing, as she was heavy in cub and the extra weight made her gasp for air. She looked this way and that as she could hear the hounds drawing ever closer. Scar, the leader of the pack was having little difficulty in following her scent that lay heavy on the frosty ground. The pack was stretched out along the embankment with the huntsmen behind. On and on the vixen ran, desperately seeking any cover in which to hide. Her tongue was hanging out of the side of her mouth and her side heaved with the effort of breathing.

Suddenly, as she passed a blackthorn thicket that was covered in frost-laden spider's webs that glistened in the sun, she picked up the strong scent of another fox that appeared to cross her path. She continued on but with every pace the distance between her and Scar was closing. The huntsmen, resplendent in their "Reds", were behind the pack that had now come down from the embankment and were strung out in a line along the fence at the bottom of it with Scar at the head. A train passed by, spilling its smoke over the pack and the field behind just as Scar reached the scent of the second fox. He left the vixen's scent and began to follow the new one. The remainder of the pack followed and began running around in circles in the field at the crossover point of the two scents. Suddenly Scar, who was still following the new scent, gave a loud haunting cry and the rest of the pack began to follow him. The huntsmen dropped in behind the pack that was now in full cry again.

The vixen ran on. Nearing exhaustion it was a while before she realised that the hounds and the hunt were fading away behind Beaconview Farm. She slowed to a walk and as the sound of the hunt disappeared into the distance she dropped down into some grass to rest. Her beautiful red coat was wet and steamed in the bright sunlight. Another train passed by, its smoke enveloping the resting fox.

While she rested, the fox that the hounds were chasing had evaded the pack by swimming across the canal. He was a large dog fox and the father of the vixen's unborn cubs. He had been well ahead of the hounds when he reached the water, and swam along the canal for quite a distance before exiting on the opposite bank. The pack cast around on the towpath of the canal desperately trying to pick up the scent but they were unsuccessful and eventually the "whipper in" gathered up the pack and they rode off in search of another fox. The dog fox lay in the sun to dry off.

Later the same day the vixen returned to her earth and the following night gave birth to three tiny cubs, two vixens and a dog called Tarn. He was the largest of the cubs as they snuggled into their mother's fur and suckled. This was the vixen's fourth litter and motherhood came naturally to her. She tended to them constantly for three days before leaving them briefly to go off and feed. Her mate left a dead rabbit at the entrance to the earth about a week after the cubs were born but that was his only visit. The cubs grew rapidly on the vixen's rich milk and as the warmer days of March arrived she would leave the cubs for brief periods and go hunting. It was during one of these excursions that the earth received an unwelcome visitor.

The vixen had left early one evening having carefully covered the cubs with bedding. Further along the embankment a stoat was hunting through the undergrowth. It's long lithe body was twisting around, occasionally sitting bolt upright and scenting the air with its pointed snout. Suddenly he picked up the scent of fox coming from a nearby bramble and without hesitation the fearless hunter entered and came upon the entrance to the earth. He went in and began to descend to where the defenceless cubs were laying, spurred on by the strong scent that was reaching his nostrils. Just at this moment the vixen returned and, sensing the presence of the stoat, rushed down the tunnel and reached the cubs at the same time as the stoat. The vixen bared her teeth at the stoat that turned and tried to rush past her. With lightning reactions the vixen spun around, grabbed the hunter by the neck and tossed it into the air, its limp body hitting the roof of the earth and dropping lifeless to the floor. After checking that the cubs were alright she carried the dead body away from the earth. That was a narrow escape for Tarn and his siblings.

With constant attention from the vixen the cubs grew quickly and within a short period were becoming active inside the earth.

Their first venture into the great wide world came one morning while the vixen was away. Sunlight was cascading through the bramble to the earth's entrance. The cubs could see the light at the end of the tunnel and curiosity drove them to move closer and closer to it. Tarn was the biggest and boldest of the three and he was the first to peer gingerly out of the entrance, eyes blinking in the bright sunlight. Suddenly a train thundered past and all three cubs scampered back down to the safety of the earth. They had felt the vibrations of the trains from within the earth but this was a whole new experience.

Life was good for the cubs, as they grew used to the world outside. Although still suckling, the vixen would bring in tasty morsels that she would leave at the earth's entrance. One evening she had left and the cubs were lying in a line with their heads resting on the floor at the entrance to the earth. Suddenly they heard a rustle in the undergrowth nearby and thinking it was the vixen they leapt to their feet just as a fox appeared through the bramble. The cubs stood apprehensively as their father approached; it was their first meeting. Tarn stepped forward cautiously and his nose met the cold wet nose of his father who looked down at the cub. The two vixen cubs followed Tarn's initiative. Their father stood impassive as the cubs sniffed at him, he looked at all three for some time before disappearing as quickly as he had come. This was the only time that the cubs were to see their father. Shortly afterwards the vixen returned and immediately sensed that her mate had visited. The cubs appeared a little restless for a few days after his visit.

As the warmth of the spring arrived, there was new growth everywhere with cowslips in profusion along the embankment. The blackthorn thickets were pure white with blossom and violets grew in small patches towards the bottom of the embankment. In the orchard at Beaconview Farm blossom was bursting out on the trees. Birds all around were busy courting and building nests. The air was full of bird song from the song thrush, blackbird and robin and these were joined by the early summer migrants such as the chiffchaff, willow warbler and blackcap. All this new activity and the different sounds fascinated the young foxes. There was so much to learn but play was their priority - running in and out of the cowslips, playing tag, leaping up onto the ant hills for King of the Castle, chasing each other's tails, play fighting, grappling together and rolling down the embankment only to run up and start again.

However, they always scampered back to the safety of the earth when a train passed only to re-emerge after it had gone and the smoke had drifted away. Life was carefree and full of fun for the three youngsters but a nervous time for the vixen as danger was all around.

One morning the vixen was resting after a night of hunting. She was a short distance from the earth lying in the warm sun. The cubs were scampering around her, leaping over her and grabbing at her brush. Tarn would go behind her, crouch down and "stalk" her tail, creeping closer and closer until suddenly he would leap at the white tipped end. As he did so, she would flick it away and he would end up with a mouthful of grass. He was learning to hunt by stealth and was becoming more successful in grabbing the brush. The two vixen cubs were more interested in play. High in the sky, drifting on outstretched wings, a buzzard was watching the cubs as it slowly began to lose height. It drifted away from the foxes as it folded its wings and gained speed. It sped along the embankment its eyes fixed on its target. Suddenly, a blackbird burst out of a bush as the buzzard sped past, its alarm call immediately alerting the vixen to the rapidly approaching danger. She snapped a warning to the playing cubs who immediately rushed for the safety of the bramble and the earth within. The buzzard swept in, focused on one of the vixen cubs and lowered its talon-loaded feet to snatch the cub. The bird was not prepared for what happened next. The cub's mother leapt into the air at the bird, striking its huge wing hard. This threw the bird completely off balance and in that split second the cub was safe, as the bird crashed into the undergrowth beyond the bramble. The vixen raced around the bramble to press home her attack but the buzzard had recovered and took off, swooping down the embankment on outstretched wings before flying across the canal and then banking around over the railway line and out of sight. The vixen returned to the cubs and found all three trembling at the very bottom of the earth, it was a few days before their courage returned to venture out and away from the earth again.

As the days started to get warmer and the cubs grew, they became more independent and adventurous. They were playing further and further away from the earth amongst the tall willow herb and nettles that grew in clumps all along the embankment. Their rough and tumble play was becoming rougher, particularly on the part of Tarn who would leap on his two siblings, nipping them hard. He even tried it on his mother but was sent away with a very sore leg from a sharp nip, the pain was a serious reminder that she was still the boss.

It was only a matter of time before they discovered the railway track itself. The smell of creosote and steel had kept them away but as they grew more adventurous, curiosity had won over. It was while the three cubs were playing tag around and through a dense clump of willow herb further down the embankment that Tarn found himself on the loose gravel on the edge of the track. He stood nervously ready to leap back into the undergrowth. The two vixen cubs followed but stayed further back, only their heads peering out from the willow herb at this strange area of steel and foul smelling wood. A large dragonfly flew low over their heads sending all three scampering back into the safety of the undergrowth only to return again shortly. This was an area worth exploring.

It was Tarn who first ventured out onto the track, nervously picking his way over the steel lines and the wooden sleepers with nose down trying to pick up any scent, but all he could smell was the creosote. His siblings followed nervously, this was a whole new world but they were curious. There was no cover on the track and they continuously looked around for danger but as their confidence increased they grew braver and started investigating along the track. Suddenly all three heard a strange sound coming from the steel track and they scampered off back into the safety of the trackside cover. What they had heard was the approaching rumble of a train, which thundered past them sending the cubs racing back to the earth.

The vixen returned shortly with a chicken stolen from the orchard at Beaconview Farm. The vixen was regularly hunting during the day to satisfy the cubs' growing appetites. They were almost weaned. Chickens, ducks and geese were all roaming free in the orchard and were an easy option for the vixen who was exploiting the food supply more and more. She was an experienced and clever fox but her predatory instinct was bringing her into conflict with the farmer, Tom Wright. He was aware that he was losing birds and was determined to stop the fox by any means.

A few days later after a very hot, sunny day the vixen was well rested and as the evening cooled she ventured off. The sun was setting and the moon beginning to rise above the distant hills. She came down from the embankment onto the towpath and entered Beaconview orchard. She searched the orchard but could find no stragglers; the birds were all safely locked up for the night in large wheeled carriages dotted around the orchard. Near the farmhouse she found a small wooden triangular ark-shaped hut surrounded by a pen of wire mesh. She could scent live birds within and started to dig under the hut. The orchard soil near the house was damp and easy to dig and within a short time she was inside. In the frenzy and confusion that followed she killed all the birds in the ark and the hut itself was overturned while Rex the farm dog barked inside the house. The fox left with a white duck and the cubs fed well that night.

The birds that the vixen had killed were sick and injured birds that Tom's grandson was looking after. When they discovered the carnage the following morning, Tom decided that this fox must be stopped at all costs and decided to set a trap to achieve this. A few nights after the vixen's visit the plans were made. A dead chicken was placed in the grass in the orchard close to the derelict lock keeper's cottage. Tom was armed with his double-barrelled shotgun and he waited with his grandson in a nearby henhouse.

The vixen had been with the cubs all day, fine-tuning their hunting skills but they still had a lot to learn. Despite the cubs' developing hunting skills the vixen continued to hunt alone although Tarn would often follow her only to lose her in the night. As the moon began to rise the vixen slipped away to hunt. Tarn tried to follow her but a sharp snap from her sent him scampering back to the earth. Unperturbed he ventured off to try again. He traced her scent down the embankment and onto the towpath but then lost it. He wandered along the path past the orchard where his mother was searching for food and up to the lock gates beyond the farm.

Meanwhile the vixen had picked up the scent of the dead chicken and was cautiously approaching in the dim glow cast over the area from the light fixed to the garage wall next to the old cottage known as Seabrook. She was approaching from behind the henhouse unaware of the two people inside. She slowly crept past the henhouse and there ahead she could see the dead hen lying on the grass. She crept towards the meal not knowing that two barrels were now trained on her. She reached the bird, smelt it, looked up and checked for danger. As she reached down and picked up the bird, she turned to move when a loud bang shattered the silence and the vixen was dead, lying where she had stood with the chicken still in her mouth.

Tarn, startled by the bang, ran along the towpath past the lock gates to a road bridge. He carried on along the road, over the canal and across the fields towards Ivinghoe Beacon. The vixen cubs were on the embankment playing with glow-worms that were displaying their luminescent bodies in the tall willow herb when the shot rang out. They ran back to the earth and cowered at the bottom, shaking. Tarn continued running in a large arc away from Beaconview, eventually up onto the embankment and back to the safety of the earth where his two siblings were still trembling. After a brief greeting all three waited expectantly for the return of the vixen with food.

As the sun rose, its rays cascaded through the bramble onto the three cubs that were at the earth's entrance. They eagerly awaited their mother as they were becoming hungry. Mid-morning, human and dog scent reached them as Tom's grandson and his dog, a brown labrador called Rex, walked along the edge of the field by the fence at the bottom of the embankment. The boy appeared to be looking up at the slope but the earth was well concealed in the bramble, the vixen had chosen her site well.

The boy and Rex passed by unaware of the cubs watching. A short while later they returned and as they did, Rex suddenly caught the faint scent of fox and stopped suddenly. The boy looked but could not see anything and walked on dragging the reluctant dog behind him. He did not know of the scent that Rex had picked up. The boy knew that the dead vixen had cubs and he was desperately trying to find them but he never did.

The cubs waited all through the hot sunny day for the return of the vixen with food but as night fell and the moon rose the three ventured out themselves. Tarn led the way. The vixens remained near the earth's entrance but Tarn went up onto the railway line and caught a mouse before darting back into the safety of the willow herb. At that moment a train thundered past, its smoke giving off a glow in the moonlight. The vixens made do with a few grubs, which they found in the dry grass.

As the days since the death of the vixen passed, the routine for the three cubs remained the same. They stayed in the earth during the scorching hot days emerging only late in the evening to hunt in the cool night air. Tarn was venturing further from the earth on his own. The vixens were less adventurous but were learning to fend for themselves initially making do with grubs and insects but mice were soon on the menu.

Each night all three would return to the earth before dawn, however one morning Tarn failed to arrive. He had wandered down off the embankment onto the towpath, past Beaconview and across the lock gates where he leapt on and killed an unsuspecting water vole. He had then wandered off towards the Ivinghoe Road. A startled heron flew up from the canal bank ahead of him, its wings appearing huge in the moonlight.

On reaching the road bridge and wary of all the strange scents, Tarn crept gingerly up the bank onto the road and cautiously crossed over the bridge. He went down onto the towpath just as car lights pierced the night sky as it approached the bridge. The startled fox raced along the towpath as the car passed over the bridge and roared away. Tarn continued running past two narrow boats moored up for the night. The strong smell of human and dog reached Tarn and as he passed the second boat a black and white Jack Russell terrier, who had been asleep on the roof, suddenly awoke and started barking and growling excitedly, straining with all its might on the chain that held it fast. A shout came from within the boat as Tarn disappeared through the hedge and into the field where cows quietly lay chewing the cud. As Tarn ran on he could hear the dog barking in the distance. He ran past the pond in the field, back onto the towpath to the swing bridge where he crossed to the other side. He sat under a tall hawthorn bush near the bridge still listening to the terrier way off in the distance. He curled up and rested for the remainder of the night and throughout the following day. This was his first night away from the shelter of the earth.

The following night he returned to the earth, but the vixens were nowhere to be seen. Having caught a mouse he settled in the earth but his siblings did not return. He remained at the earth for a few days but was alone. Then, after a particularly good hunting session, he slept all day under a large hawthorn bush near the swing bridge and that was the beginning of his independent life. Over the next few weeks he remained in the vicinity of the embankment, canal and Beaconview Farm. He was building up a good mental picture of his territory and it was this knowledge that was to save his life more than once in the future.

A site that Tarn soon found on one of his forays was an old straw rick in a field near the towpath beyond the Ivinghoe Road bridge. The rick was formed of bales of straw that were old and rotten, the rick itself partly collapsed. This was an excellent hunting ground for rats and mice and became a regular spot for Tarn.

On one occasion he had eaten well and had settled down deep in a crevice between two bales. The air was hot and humid as a storm built in the west. The huge dark menacing clouds had already smothered the moon as they came racing in on the increasing wind. Suddenly there was a bright flash of lightning, almost immediately followed by a loud crack of thunder. Tarn moved back deep into the crevice as the torrential rain came sweeping across the field and over the rick. With his brush under his chin and his head on his front paws he watched the storm. Forked lightning raced across the sky, lighting up his eyes, closely followed by cracks of thunder, as the storm seemed to linger for some time. The rain came down in torrents but he was dry deep inside the rick. The storm raged through the night but as dawn broke it drifted east, the dark clouds obscuring the sunrise above Ivinghoe Beacon. The rumbles of thunder grew fainter. The storm left the air cool and fresh but Tarn had no desire to move.

Unbeknown to the fox, Rex and the boy were approaching the rick from along the towpath. Besides being a good source of food for the fox, Rex enjoyed hunting there and was straining on his lead to get amongst the bales. The boy climbed over the wire and through a hole in the hedge into the field before slipping the dog's lead. Rex ran towards the rick and almost immediately Tarn was alerted as the dog's scent reached him. The dog was approaching from behind the rick. Tarn crept out of his crevice and into the field. The boy, who was still some way off, spotted him but Rex was so busy excitedly hunting through the straw that he did not see the retreating fox. Tarn burst into a run and turned in a big arc back to the hedge and the towpath beyond. He ran for some distance before he felt safe. Tarn was to have many more encounters with humans and the dangers they posed.

Soon after this close encounter with the boy and Rex, Tarn was to have an experience that involved an animal that he was to learn to respect.

Late one summer evening the sun had set and the full moon was high in the sky above Ivinghoe Beacon, Tarn stirred from his resting place deep in a bramble on the south-facing embankment. The hot sun had cascaded down through the branches onto the resting fox, who was well concealed and rested. He stretched, yawned and scratched behind his ear. He scented the air for danger just as a train thundered past, its smoke cascading down the embankment and over him, its acrid smell ruining any chance of picking up any danger signals.

He wandered down the embankment and into the field where the ginger Suffolk Punch was gently grazing on the opposite side of the field. Tarn strolled slowly across the field, through the hedge and into the lane where he suddenly picked up the strong scent of human. He cowered down into the undergrowth and froze as the man cycled past in the direction of the village. As the man disappeared into the night Tarn crossed the lane into the wheat field and the safety of cover. He walked through the field searching for an unwary harvest mouse but was unlucky. Eventually he emerged through the hedge onto Spinney Hill. The sheep were all on the far side of the hill, some lying down, others grazing quietly.

He was walking up the hill in the shadow of the hedge towards the spinney when suddenly another scent reached him that stopped him in his tracks. It was a scent that he did not recognise and it seemed to be coming from the direction of the spinney. He continued on cautiously and entered the spinney through a thick bed of stinging nettles that surrounded the small clump of trees. He then passed under the wire fence that kept the sheep out. The moonlight was filtering through the trees forming curious shadows on the ground. The scent was growing stronger as he moved. He stopped and crouched down nervously as a strange snuffling sound reached his ears. The instinct to run was strong but curiosity was stronger. The sound was getting closer and closer to him. A tawny owl landed on silent wings on a branch of a tree above the fox and the bird looked down at Tarn who was unaware that he was under scrutiny.

The sound grew closer until suddenly in a small clearing just ahead of the fox, a black and white striped face appeared, its pointed nose rooting around in the soil. A young badger was busy looking for food and did not notice Tarn until the fox stood up. This momentarily startled the badger who froze and stared at him. Both youngsters stood staring, the silence only broken by the hoot of the owl above them, this appeared to break the standoff. The badger was hungry so it shuffled off past Tarn who watched it intently as it disappeared into the nettles. It reappeared shortly afterwards in the grass on the hill, out of sight of the fox who began to follow the badger's scent at a discreet distance. He crept through the nettles, under the wire and onto the hill. The badger ignored him and continued searching for food in the short grass. Tarn could not understand this curious creature and followed it at a safe distance sniffing the air with eyes fixed firmly on the badger.

Suddenly the badger stopped, turned and ran towards Tarn, grunting. He leapt sideways as the badger rushed past him, before turning and running at him again. His turn of speed far outmatched that of the badger. He ran forward, stopped and turned to see where the badger was. To his surprise it was not far behind him. He again leapt sideways but this time the badger was ready and nipped him on his leg. Tarn sprung into the air as he leapt away. The nip did not hurt and he went on the attack. He rushed at the badger. Startled by the change of role the badger stood his ground and snapped at the fox who swung sideways before reaching his opponent. This was a good game; the two animals were running around in skittish fun. The fox running past the badger who would snap at his legs, then the badger would chase the fox in a tight circle. Both animals were so absorbed in the game that neither had seen the owl flying overhead, looking down at them as it disappeared into the night. Nor had they noticed the sheep and lambs that had got to their feet and were watching the two with some curiosity. The two young creatures were totally absorbed with the play and oblivious to everything around them. Running and leaping they played on for quite a while, their shadows dancing on the grass.

As suddenly as the game had started, it stopped, with both creatures panting heavily. They glanced at each other and the badger trotted off back to the cover of the spinney. Tarn began to follow his newfound friend but a disgruntled ewe chased him; he ran down the hill to the hedge and the safety of the tall wheat beyond. The moon's reflection was shimmering on the canal's surface as he reached the towpath. He trotted along the path under the road bridge just as a train shattered the peace by thundering over the iron bridge beyond. The smoke appeared to shine in the moonlight as it drifted down the embankment.

An unwary water vole made a welcome meal. Tarn passed under the iron bridge and across the swing bridge beyond to the opposite side of the water. He finally settled under the tall hawthorn bush near the canal bank and rested; the play with the badger had sapped his energy.

Life for the next few weeks was fairly routine for Tarn, hunting at night and resting up during the day. The hot summer drifted on and the crops in the fields around Beaconview were ripening. The wheat in the field at the bottom of Spinney Hill was now a golden brown and full of harvest mice, which Tarn found difficult to catch. One night after an unsuccessful hunting foray, he decided to rest up in the wheat field. While the sun came up in the east heralding another hot day the skylarks rose in the blue sky, their song cascading over the resting Tarn who was blissfully unaware of the approaching danger that was unfolding all around him.

Men had started work on the edge of the field with a machine harvesting the wheat. They had already completed the first swathe around the headland of the field and the harvested wheat was tied in sheaves and left standing in clumps ready for loading onto the trailer at the end of the harvest. Tarn continued to sleep in the hot sun, deep within the crop while swallows skimmed across the surface of the wheat immediately above him catching insects. A kestrel dropped onto an escaping harvest mouse that was exposed in the stubble.

Suddenly Tarn heard a noise and the sound of humans in the distance. He leapt to his feet and skulked off away from the sound but as he did so he became confused, as the sound was moving. He changed direction again and again in an attempt to escape the approaching danger. The scent of humans and the acrid smell of steel had now reached him as he was running through the wheat. Another young kestrel was watching the frightened fox who was desperately trying to make good his escape but on reaching the edge of the standing wheat and being confronted with the increasing expanse of stubble he would turn back and run to another side. On one occasion he was spotted by one of the men and a gun was loaded in readiness.

Fear was now gripping Tarn who was young and inexperienced. He continued to run within the wheat, but the area of cover was reducing all the time. The sounds of the machines and men were drawing ever closer. Tarn crouched down as close to the ground as he could and trembled; his ears flat to his head that rested on the soil, his eyes wide with fear and confusion. The machine that was cutting the wheat passed by within feet of the terrified fox but he remained unseen by the men who followed it. As the danger passed him he raised himself up and skulked off along the narrow strip of standing wheat remaining at the edge but he was still not prepared to leave the cover of the crop. He sat tight, trembling as the men reached the end of the line they were cutting and commenced the final strip, with one man walking alongside the machine, his gun at the ready.

A hare broke cover ahead of the machine. There was a loud bang and the creature was dead, a second shot rang out almost immediately as the other barrel discharged its lethal load into a fleeing rabbit. Tarn had dropped into a low crouch at the far end of the strip. A scurrying rat startled him as it ran past into the stubble and disappeared into a nearby stack of sheaves. The machine was drawing closer until it appeared to be on top of him. As the long cutting blade was about to sever his brush Tarn bolted out of the wheat, his ears flat, and ran as fast as he could. One of the men shouted and almost immediately there was a loud bang and Tarn felt the lead shot whistle past his head and crash into a stack of sheaves next to him.

He ran on and the second shot rang out this time slamming into the ground immediately behind him. By the time the gun was reloaded he was through the hedge onto Spinney Hill and running at full pace through the sheep. The man with the gun cursed his luck; Tarn had had a very narrow escape indeed.

Once in the cover of the spinney Tarn stopped running, panting heavily with the exertion and heat. He sat down nervously. The men in the field had finished harvesting the crop and were now busy loading the sheaves onto a low trailer to take back to the farm. As the sun set behind

Spinney Hill the last of the sheaves were cleared from the small field.

Tarn rested up in the spinney for the remainder of the day and when the moon was high in the sky he stirred from his cover. He stretched, yawned and, feeling hungry, wandered out of the wood in search of food. He passed through the hedge back into the field where he had almost lost his life only a short while ago. The field seemed strange, the sharp stubble hurting his legs. He kept close to the hedge as he skirted around the edge of the field until he reached the canal. He trotted along to the road bridge on the towpath, went up the track and onto the bridge itself. He crossed over and picked up a few morsels around the tables outside the Duke of Wellington then re-crossed the bridge, hunting along the path to Beaconview Farm. On reaching the swing bridge he crossed the canal, the moon casting Tarn's shadow on the surface of the water below him. He rested up under the tall familiar hawthorn bush near the canal bank; a cow lying nearby threw him a cursory glance and continued chewing the cud unperturbed.

Until his narrow escape Tarn had had little contact with humans but having survived the shotgun he was to remain very wary of them in the future.

One morning Tarn was in the field adjacent to the large Nissen hut at Beaconview Farm. He was on his way back to the hawthorn bush after a night of hunting. The sun was high and skylarks were singing enthusiastically. The sunlight shimmered on the water surface, which ruffled in the breeze. Unbeknown to Tarn, the boy was on the towpath just beyond the hedge. As Tarn reached the hedge and passed through it onto the path, he turned towards the swing bridge and immediately caught sight of the boy. Tarn froze, startled and momentarily confused. The two stared at each other. The boy was perfectly still and as his scent reached Tarn's nostrils this seemed to bring the fox to his senses. He leapt back through the hedge and ran flat out past the cows grazing in the field who took no notice of the fleeing fox.

With the ponds and the canal being such a prominent part of Tarn's territory, it was not long before he had his first real experience of water. It was early one autumn evening; the sun had set and the stars were beginning to appear. Tarn had set off early to hunt and was in the field near the Nissen hut. He was skirting around the pond, when he suddenly caught the scent of duck. A pair of mallards were asleep on the trunk of a willow tree that hung out almost horizontally over the surface of the pond. Their heads were tucked deep into the plumage on their backs. Tarn spotted them and crouched down tight to the ground.

With slow deliberate movements he began to creep very slowly towards the ducks. He reached the tree and with little difficulty moved over the root ball on the bank and up onto the trunk. Slowly and silently he crept along the tree and out over the water towards the sleeping mallards, his body tense with excitement. Suddenly, with only a few feet separating predator and prey, a moorhen flew out from under the tree squawking in alarm. The ducks stirred and immediately took flight on seeing the fox. In his excitement and confusion Tarn leapt off the tree in a vain attempt to catch one of the airborne ducks. He sailed through the air for some distance before crashing into the water in the centre of the pond with a loud splash. He submerged momentarily before bobbing back to the surface and kicking out wildly with all four legs.

He swam to the bank and his bedraggled form emerged from the water. Covered in pondweed and strands of watercress he looked a sorry sight. He shook himself and rolled in the grass to remove the weed that was clinging to his coat. His ears were full of water and this irritated him; he shook his head violently to clear them. He skulked off to the hedge by the canal where he licked his coat and removed the green algae that was matted into his fur. His coat took a while to dry in the cool autumn night air.

Soon after the experience with the ducks Tarn was to enter the water unintentionally for a second time. He was walking along the towpath below the lock gates one wet and windy night. The wind was whipping up the surface of the canal into a frenzy and howling through the hedge. Suddenly a water vole scurried across the path a few feet ahead of Tarn and stopped momentarily on a tussock of grass overhanging the water. Tarn leapt at the rodent, missed it and went headlong into the canal. The water vole had slipped into the water and was swimming away under the surface below Tarn who was swimming back to the bank. However on reaching the edge he was unable to pull himself out, as the bank at this point was too steep. He swam along the edge of the bank for quite a distance before he found a spot where he could haul himself out. He shook himself violently but the rain was so heavy that it made little difference. A sudden flash of lightning heralded another storm. Tarn crossed the lock gate, a dangerous undertaking in the wind, and took shelter under the big oak tree. He stayed there until the sun was high in the sky the following day and lay in the sun drying his coat out. He had learned to respect water.

Since leaving the vixen cubs at the earth, Tarn had not met another fox but that was to change one night in late autumn. He had been hunting in the spinney on the hill and was walking leisurely back towards the railway line when suddenly he picked up the scent of another fox on the strong breeze. Another fox in his territory was not to be tolerated and he began to follow the scent, which appeared to be coming from the direction of the canal. He ran into the breeze with ears pricked and brush held high. He drew closer to the source of the scent; Briar the vixen was on the towpath and was unaware of the approaching dog fox. Tarn was now running fast towards the hedge by the towpath, there was something about the scent that was exciting him, a feeling that he had not felt before.

On reaching the hedge he burst through onto the towpath a few feet ahead of Briar. Both foxes stopped in their tracks and glared at each other, motionless. Briar was larger than Tarn and although she was older than him she had not yet raised a family. She was resplendent in her winter coat having moulted earlier whereas Tarn had just begun his moult.

Suddenly Briar raced forward at Tarn who ran off startled along the towpath towards Beaconview. Under the railway bridge, both foxes stopped as a train thundered past overhead. Briar ran off the way they had come and Tarn began to chase her. They ran back to the hump-backed bridge by the Duke of Wellington, which they had raced under shortly before. Briar stopped in her tracks so quickly that Tarn almost crashed into her. She snarled and snapped at him, catching him on the front leg. In an attempt to avoid her he leapt through the hedge into the field beyond but Briar pressed home the attack and chased him around the field. She nipped Tarn's back leg and the pain spurred him on. He ran in a big semi-circle rejoining the towpath by the railway bridge. He continued to run along the path under the bridge and past the orchard at the farm.

Briar was still hot on his heels, snapping viciously at his legs and brush, giving him several painful nips. Both foxes were giving out high-pitched barks and screams and the noise awoke Rex who had been asleep outside Seabrook. As the two foxes raced past the gate Rex burst onto the path barking excitedly and startling both of them. All three ran up to the lock gates and the two foxes ran in a small circle back towards the farm and the railway bridge.

Rex was close behind Briar but Tarn was well ahead of them both. Past the gate he ran, into the farm and the orchard beyond. Tarn saw that the swing bridge was across the canal so on reaching it he leapt up onto the boards and raced across. Briar ran past the bridge and Rex continued chasing her. Tarn ran across the field between the cows and heard the dog's barks slowly disappearing into the distance as the fox and dog having passed under the railway bridge were in the field and running towards Spinney Hill.

Tarn slowed to a trot; his legs were sore from Briar's nips. He walked up onto the top of the embankment and looked across towards Spinney Hill just as Rex stopped barking. A train thundered past just feet from where Tarn was standing. He curled up half way down the embankment in a patch of tall dead willow herb and slept; he had had enough excitement for one night.

So Tarn's early life was full of encounters and experiences with many lessons learned which were to hold him in good stead as his life developed. His first winter was to prove to be a good test of those lessons along with the knowledge of his territory and the continued threat from humans.

# Chapter Two
## GROWING UP

As the winter set in with long, cold nights and short days, Tarn became more and more restless; he wanted a mate. He revisited Ivinghoe Beacon twice more in an attempt to find Briar and although her scent was strong on the top of the hill he could not find her earth. Hunting was more difficult now with the freezing nights and he was spending more time seeking food - the rotten straw rick had very few rats left. He had even visited the orchard at Beaconview but there were no unwary chickens.

One night Tarn made a gruesome discovery whilst hunting the railway track. He was heading towards Cheddington village and a bitterly cold north-easterly wind was blowing into his dense winter coat. Near the football pitch, he came upon the body of a fox lying by the side of the track. He approached it cautiously and sniffed at it. The dead fox had been struck by a train, it was one of the vixens from his earth and her contorted body was covered in blood. The sound of an oncoming train reverberated down the steel track and Tarn slipped away into a bramble nearby. He continued on along the embankment behind a row of houses at the edge of the village.

Exciting scents suddenly reached his nostrils that made him come down from the embankment. Amongst them was a strong scent of human but hunger drove him. He ran across a strip of scrub and into the back garden of one of the houses. Cautiously he approached the house and found a dustbin from where the delicious scent was coming; there was no lid. Tarn sprung up with his front feet onto the rim but he could not reach inside. There was no alternative, if he wanted the food he would have to jump up into the bin itself. With one leap he was inside the bin and in a second had grabbed the cooked turkey carcass. Getting out of the almost empty bin was not so easy as getting in. Try as he might, the carcass firmly held in his jaws stopped him getting out, but with one huge leap the bin fell over with a loud crash. Tarn ran along the alley by the side of the house and out into the road at the front. As he did so he heard the side door of the house open and the sound of human voices. He ran off down the street towards the centre of the village. On reaching the school he went through the gates into the playground and through to the back where he sheltered out of the wind in a small lean-to to eat his prize.

The wind had grown even stronger by the time he emerged from the school onto the footpath. He trotted back along the path the way he had come to the edge of the village. In many of the gardens there were strange lights hanging in the trees and swaying madly in the wind. They were also in the windows of some of the houses. Some of the lights were flashing on and off. At The Swan public house a tall fir tree in the front car park was covered in these lights, which were flashing and swaying, lighting up the cold dark night sky. Tarn had not taken much notice of these lights as he had run down the road with his food but they now made him nervous as he ran along the path out of the village. He passed through a gate and went up onto Spinney Hill where the gusting wind hit him hard and almost knocked him off his feet. The sheep on the hill were sensibly in the shelter of the spinney. Tarn passed through them and they took little notice. He entered the spinney under the barbed wire fence and was soon out of the wind. Thankfully the badger was sensibly asleep deep in his sett. Tarn rested deep in a bramble as the wind continued through the night.

The following morning Tarn awoke with a start to the sound of the church bells pealing out across the countryside. The cold wind had dropped to a breeze but was still in the northeast as Tarn emerged from the spinney and surveyed the countryside below him. The little road was quiet; a train passed by spewing its smoke down the embankment before it drifted on the breeze. Two narrow boats were moored up on the canal by the bridge at the Duke of Wellington and smoke drifted up from their chimneys. Tarn stretched and yawned and had a good scratch before moving off down the line of the hedge to the road.

The church bells were still ringing when he crossed the little road and wandered up the lane leading to Beaconview. Instead of passing under the bridge he went up the side onto the embankment just as another train thundered past enveloping him in smoke. He pounced on an unwary mouse, before crossing the railway track and settling in a patch of bramble and resting for the remainder of the day.

As dusk fell the wind increased again and the temperature dropped dramatically. The wind was penetrating the bramble so Tarn wandered along the embankment to the old earth. It had a layer of dead leaves in the bottom but it was sound and comparatively warm out of the wind that howled outside.

The next morning the wind was as strong as ever and the sky was grey and heavy. Driven by hunger Tarn ventured out of the earth onto the towpath. He was unaware of the assembly of humans that were gathering in front of The Swan public house. Horseboxes had started to arrive early, parking up at various locations through the village, and a number were on the village green near the school. The horses were being brought out, groomed and having their manes and tails plaited ready for the hunt.

By mid-morning the riders had begun to gather at the pub, the huntsmen resplendent in their 'Pinks'. Trays of drinks and hot mince pies were being handed around but some of the huntsmen were inside the pub enjoying a festive drink out of the bitter wind that had veered around to the east. One or two flakes of snow were blowing in the wind. Eventually the hunt master came out of the pub and mounted his horse. He was retired Colonel Charles Foster-Smythe - an elderly man with many years experience of hunting Tarn's ancestors. The 'whipper in' brought the hounds into a tight pack through the village and joined the hunt at the pub. The leader of the pack was Scar, who was now a seasoned campaigner. With everyone now ready and numerous onlookers from the village on the pavements, the master led the hunt through the village and on to Mentmore Towers where they were to draw the first piece of cover. The snow was slowly increasing as Scar and the hounds cast for scent.

Tarn had reached the old straw rick and was waiting motionless for an unwary rat, there were still a few in amongst the rotting straw. Suddenly one appeared - a quick dash by Tarn and the rat was dead in his jaws. As he sat in a hole in the straw out of the wind, the scent of human reached his nostrils. He crouched down low as the boy and Rex passed by on the towpath back towards Beaconview.

The hunt was drawing through some dense cover in Mentmore Park when Scar suddenly gave out an eerie cry - he had picked up the fresh scent of a fox. In fact it was the scent of Briar who, on hearing the approaching hunt, had dashed out of a deep bramble where she had rested overnight and was heading across a field towards the railway station, directly into the wind. The hounds found it easy to follow her and were in full cry. The 'field', led by the master, were close behind in full gallop. The snow was falling heavily now, almost horizontal in the strong wind, which blew directly into the faces of Briar, the hounds and the riders.

Briar was at full stretch as she reached the hedge. She darted through a small hole in the base, over the road and up a track between two orchards leading to the Church. Scar and the pack were close behind. Through the churchyard Briar ran, weaving in and out of the gravestones. She dashed into the open field beyond leading down to the railway line. Way off in the distance almost obscured by the snow was the peak of Ivinghoe Beacon. Briar ran on, the hounds losing her scent in the churchyard and casting around desperately trying to find it, the falling snow not helping them. Scar had drifted out into the field with another very experienced hound. Suddenly he gave out the same eerie cry and the chase was back on. In that short space of time, Briar had gained a lot of ground and was just passing under the fence by the railway line, as the pack were running down the field from the church. She went up on to the track and ran along for a short while before running down the embankment the other side just as a train thundered past. Its smoke was blown with the heavy falling snow towards the hounds that were in full cry once again.

Briar was running along the base of the embankment. As the hounds reached the line and crossed over, they again lost her scent momentarily. Out of sight of the hounds, Briar ran back over the line, down the embankment and ran along the base again for a short distance before crossing the track again. However this time she ran out into the field and off towards the Ivinghoe road. The effect of crossing the track as Briar had done, had thrown the hounds into confusion and it was a long time before they regained her scent in the field once more. Briar had managed to gain some distance from the hounds. She had crossed three fields and was near to the road when she suddenly changed direction and ran towards the canal, and unknowingly towards Tarn who was resting in the hole in the straw.

Suddenly Tarn heard sounds that he had not heard before, a hunting horn way off in the distance and the cry of the hounds. He was immediately alert and piercing the air with his ears. The wind had distorted the sounds and the hunt was a lot closer than he initially realised. He sneaked away from the rick, through the hedge and onto the white footpath. He trotted along towards the Ivinghoe road and unknowingly into danger, for Briar was leading the hounds right to him. The wind was howling in Tarn's ears and he flattened them against his head, which blocked out a lot of sound including the approaching hunt.

Briar had crossed the road and was now parallel to the roadside hedge leading to the canal. She burst through the hedge a short distance ahead of Tarn on the other side of the bridge. Tarn pricked his ears up and immediately heard the sound of the pack and the hunting horn blowing nearby. He ran up the path by the side of the bridge onto the road and immediately stopped, for there on the road was the hunt. One of the leading riders spotted Tarn immediately and called loudly. Tarn spun around, ran back down the path to the canal and went like the wind along the towpath. Scar had picked him up and the chase was on. Down the path the pack tumbled with the field close behind, they were forced to ride single file along the towpath, as it was narrow in places. The hounds in their enthusiasm were falling over one another to get to the lead and twice a hound fell into the canal and had to drag itself out of the freezing cold water.

Tarn was flat out with the wind behind him. Scar was leading the pack and was close to the terrified fox. Suddenly Tarn dived through a very small hole in the hedge and ran on through the field. The hounds couldn't get through and were forced to run on till they found a gap. Tarn had built up a good distance from Scar and the pack. He ran across two more fields and past the pond behind the Nissen hut at Beaconview. He ran around the hedge by the farmhouse and out onto the lane leading to the farm. He ran around the bend, down the long stretch under the railway bridge, across the road at the bottom and into the field below Spinney Hill. The hounds were back on his scent and were closing the gap. The snow was building up on the ground and was draining the energy of both fox and hound.

Scar and the pack were just passing under the bridge as Tarn ran straight across the field towards the hill in what was now heavy, blinding, horizontal snow that stung his eyes as he ran. As he reached the far hedge, the pack burst into the field on the far side in full cry on Tarn's fresh track. He passed through the densest part of the spinney, out on to the brow of the hill and over the other side, the barren white landscape spread out before him. The pack was at the spinney and had lost Tarn's scent in the dense undergrowth. The heavy snow and driving bitter wind were making conditions difficult for Scar and his pack, but they cast around desperately seeking the familiar scent.

Tarn ran on down the hill, through some scrub and out on to the old airfield. Its surface was featureless under a deep carpet of snow; visibility for Tarn was poor for not only was the falling snow blinding him, the wind was lifting the settled snow and blowing it along the surface, coating anything in its path, including the fox. His pace had slowed as he ploughed through the deep snow. Suddenly he sank deep; the gully was full of snow. He desperately pulled himself out. He could hear the hounds behind him, above the howling wind, as they were in full cry again down the hill; Scar had re-discovered Tarn's scent and was leading the pack through the blinding snow, driven on by a primeval instinct.

Tarn continued on with head and ears down, the wind was hitting him in the side, his brush blowing in the wind. The sound of the hounds was drawing ever closer as he struggled on. They found the gully that Tarn had previously sunk into but they were soon clear of it. The huntsmen had now caught up with the pack and two of them were riding ahead either side of Tarn who had seen them but struggled on. The huntsmen were trying to turn the fox but he continued on. Suddenly, in a deep gully ahead of him that was partially full of snow, Tarn saw the opening of a drainage tunnel.

The huntsmen had also seen it and began shouting loudly at the fox to try and confuse him, but he was concentrating on reaching that tunnel. One of the huntsmen stopped his horse on the bank above the tunnel and was quickly trying to dismount in an effort to block off the tunnel entrance but Tarn made a huge leap from a deep drift on the opposite bank and landed half in the pipe before disappearing into the darkness. The huntsmen cursed as Tarn disappeared from his view. As Tarn ran along the tunnel he could hear Scar and the pack around the entrance, barking and whining in frustration, as the tunnel was too narrow for them to follow.

Tarn slowed and shook himself. He was covered in snow, his coat soaked. The tunnel was damp and cold but it was out of the wind and snow. The hounds had gone quiet far behind him but another danger was about to confront him as a terrier was placed in the tunnel to flush Tarn out. The dog immediately picked up Tarn's strong scent and began running along the tunnel, its yapping call echoed in the darkness. Tarn heard it and tried to run away from the sound. The little dog was soon closing in on the fox who increased his speed. On reaching a junction in the tunnels, Tarn swung left and ran on. The terrier was not fooled and continued to follow, barking loudly. At another junction Tarn veered right, unaware of a large rat in the opposite tunnel sheltering from the raging blizzard outside.

The rat ran off confused, he could hear the terrier but the echoing disguised which tunnel it was in. The rat ran into the tunnel that Tarn had just left straight into the path of the terrier, which saw its arch-enemy and with one quick bite to the neck and a toss against the concrete wall of the tunnel killed the rodent. The terrier spent a short while sniffing at it before resuming the chase. Tarn had gained some distance on the dog in this short time and had turned off again, more or less doubling back on himself. The terrier had slowed as the strong scent of rat was distracting him from his purpose. He killed another and another, this was a lot more fun than running after Tarn. The terrier went on a killing frenzy as he discovered many more rodents. Tarn ran on and made his escape by leaving a good distance between himself and the terrier who he could hear way off in the distance, barking excitedly.

Tarn stopped and crouched in the tunnel, the terrier was moving away from him in its excitement. At the entrance to the tunnel the terrier man was desperately calling the terrier; the hunt master had decided to call it a day. Weather conditions were now so bad that it was dangerous for the horses. All the hazards were now buried in snow and the field had been reduced to a handful of riders as many had peeled away and gone home in the atrocious conditions. The hounds were led away with the 'field', leaving the terrier man and his assistant to retrieve the terrier that they assumed was still following the fox.

Much later in the day, dusk fell and much to the relief of his owner, the blood soaked terrier emerged from the tunnel, now deep in snow. The terrier man picked him up and placed him back into his wire-fronted hunting box. He was pleased to get the terrier back and was delighted that he had killed the fox, assuming of course that that was where the blood had come from. He reported this fact back to the hunt master the following morning. The truth of course was that the terrier had had a wonderful time killing rats, which he found much more fun than chasing the fox, and it was this that had undoubtedly saved Tarn's life.

Tarn remained in the tunnel for the rest of the night, resting while the blizzard raged on. Tarn eventually made his way back down the labyrinth of tunnels, stumbling across a dead rat killed by the terrier. Tarn ate this in one gulp followed by another and another; the terrier had left a veritable larder for the fox. Eventually he emerged cautiously, through a drift that had built up at the tunnel entrance, out into brilliant sunshine. The glare of the snow momentarily blinded Tarn as he emerged from the dark tunnel. He struggled through the deep snow in the ditch, twice disappearing completely, but eventually scrambling to the top. There was no sign of where the hunt or the terrier man had been in the virgin snow; their tracks had been filled in by the blizzard. This was yet another new experience for the young fox and he pushed his nose deep into the snow that was up to his chest as he moved off. His face emerged covered in snow and he sneezed violently. He repeated it several times - this was great fun.

The landscape had been completely transformed, familiar features were buried, and the surface was flat, glaring white and glistening in the brilliant sunshine. There was very little scent on the still air. Tarn began to make his way across the airfield towards the canal. He disappeared twice in deep snowdrifts before hauling himself out and shaking. The countryside was silent, nothing stirred. Slowly and laboriously he worked his way to the canal, scrambling through a deep drift that had built up by the side of the hedge next to the towpath. Once on the path he shook himself and peered around. The surface of the canal was still and mirrored the bushes on the opposite bank. He turned towards the Duke of Wellington way off in the distance and walked towards it. The towpath had a covering of snow but it wasn't as deep as on the airfield - the hedge had caught most of it but every now and then there were deep ridges of snow across the path where it had blown through gaps in the hedge.

A startled blackbird burst out of the hedge as the fox approached. It flew across the canal and landed in a bush on the opposite bank sending snow crashing into the water, which rippled across the surface. As Tarn reached the tall willow tree that overhung the path after the swing bridge, a wood pigeon flew out of the tree sending lumps of snow cascading down onto the hapless fox, a large lump hitting his head. He shook himself and sneezed and looked at the pigeon as it disappeared across the barren white landscape. He passed Seabrook and continued on up to the lock, where he leapt gingerly up onto the gate beam and cautiously walked across to the other side; the clear, brilliant sunlight glared off the surface of the water into his face.

Under the tall oak on the opposite side, he found footprints in the snow and the scent of another fox. He spent some time searching around and following the scent that had aroused him. The track led him along the bank, past the hawthorn bush and the swing bridge and up on to the railway embankment. Passing trains had obliterated the tracks and despite searching for some time he did not find the trail. Unbeknown to him the fox had walked a considerable distance along the track. Briar had returned to the area late in the night after the blizzard had blown itself out. She was looking for a mate.

# Chapter Three
# THE RIVAL

The snow disappeared as fast as it had arrived, leaving huge cold puddles in the fields. The canal had risen to the very top of the banks but didn't flood over. A stirring within Tarn led him in search of a mate. He had found no trace of Briar since her tracks in the snow until one cold still night when he was in the fields beyond the canal towards Beacon Hill. Stars were bright in the clear winter's night and it was beginning to freeze. Suddenly the silence was shattered by the half bark - half scream of a vixen calling. Tarn's ears pricked up as a second call rang out. It was Briar calling from the direction of the hill. Tarn ran across the fields towards her. As he approached the main road he disappeared into a dense blackthorn hedge, close to the road. Cars and lorries were thundering past very closely, their lights pierced through the hedge as they went. This was a new and frightening experience for Tarn; the only traffic he had experienced was the occasional car in the quiet road leading to Cheddington.

As Tarn sat in the hedge looking at the road, Briar gave out another call that could be heard above the traffic. With instinct driving him on he dashed out of the safety of the hedge into the road. The headlights of two cars bearing down on him from opposite directions immediately lit up his form. He cleared the first but as he leapt for the hedge on the opposite side of the road the tyre of the second car glanced his brush, knocking him violently sideways. Tarn crashed into the hedge, the wind from the passing car sending him rolling over and in one move he got to his feet and leapt into the safety of the undergrowth. Shaken he was none the worse for his first interaction with a car.

Briar gave out another call; she was close to where Tarn was sitting. He crept out of the hedge into the field. Briar was on top of a hill in the field but Tarn couldn't see her. He made towards the middle of the field as Briar gave out yet another call. Tarn trotted towards her, but suddenly stopped in his tracks as her call was answered with a bark from nearby. Tarn was not the only dog fox in the field. Confused he looked around, there was Briar sitting on the hill to his right looking straight at him. He began to approach her but as he drew nearer he suddenly spotted the dog fox on the other side of the hill also approaching Briar.

The dog fox on spotting Tarn made a dash towards him, his teeth bared. Tarn ran off confused. He outran the older fox who stopped the pursuit and returned to Briar. Tarn stopped running on top of another hill and looked across towards Briar. The dog fox had stopped a short distance from her and was sitting looking at her.

Tarn watched for a short while then came down off the hill towards Briar, instinct and the desire to mate was driving him on. As he approached, the dog fox sprang to his feet and again ran towards Tarn, snapping his jaws with teeth bared. This time however Tarn stood his ground. The two met head on and rose up on their hind legs and snarled before lashing out at each other with some ferocity.

The dog fox bit Tarn's right cheek but Tarn bit his adversary's neck. The encounter was brief but vicious.

Both foxes broke off and glared at each other, panting heavily. Suddenly the dog fox launched himself at Tarn, but Tarn side stepped him and bit him hard in his flank. The dog fox turned remarkably quickly for an old fox and caught Tarn by surprise with a bite to his flank. Tarn ran clear in some pain from the bite. The dog fox pursued him for a short distance and then stopped and returned to Briar who was still sitting on the hill.

Tarn turned and ran after the dog fox that, on seeing the approaching youngster, ran off at full stretch. Tarn chased after him slowly closing in on the dog, but what the old dog fox lacked in speed he made up for with cunning. When both foxes were flat out the old dog fox suddenly stopped with apparent ease. This took Tarn completely by surprise; he tried to side-step the dog but as he did so the dog caught his right hind leg and bit hard into it. Tarn somersaulted through the air and landed on his back. The dog was on him in an instant and bit him on the muzzle and in the neck as Tarn struggled to his feet and ran off. The dog fox pursued him and bit Tarn again in the right hind leg. Tarn leapt into the air in pain and gave out a yelp. The dog fox stopped, and returned to Briar.

Tarn was in a lot of pain from his right leg but was not going to give up. As the dog fox reached Briar, Tarn suddenly hit him in the flank at full speed. Both foxes rolled over and over in the wet, young wheat snapping and snarling at each other. Eventually the dog fox ran off, startled by the ferocity of the young fox. Tarn pursued him; on and on they ran, through a hedge and up onto Ivinghoe Beacon itself. Rabbits scattered in all directions as the noisy foxes ran over their warrens. The dog fox lost his footing in one and crashed to the ground, Tarn seizing the advantage leapt on the dog fox biting him deep into his neck. The dog fox ran off as Tarn pressed home his attack.

Back through the hedge they ran into the field where Briar was still sitting. Suddenly the dog fox stopped in his tracks again so suddenly that Tarn was forced to leap over the dog fox. While in the air the dog fox reached up and bit Tarn hard and deep into his right leg. Tarn came down hard on his now bleeding leg. Both foxes glared at each other, panting heavily, their breath condensing in the cold night air. A tawny owl flew over head screeching in alarm as she glared down at the assembly below her.

The stand off lasted quite a while but was suddenly broken by a lunge from the dog fox at Tarn, who sidestepped the snapping jaws and bit the dog fox hard in the flank. Instead of pressing home his advantage the inexperienced fox ran off on his injured leg pursued by the dog fox. But this time Tarn was limping badly and was weakened by the pain from his injured right leg, blood was seeping from the wounds. Tarn stopped and side stepped the dog but he was cunning and he also side-stepped and bit Tarn deep and hard again on his right leg. Tarn collapsed on the ground in fear. His ears folded down tight against his head, he snarled in terror at the dog fox who was about to press home his attack. Both foxes glared at each other. The dog fox lunged forward at Tarn, who rolled onto his side. The dog fox went for Tarn's throat to finish him off, Tarn moved sideways and at that moment Briar gave out another call. The dog fox looked across at her, the now terrified Tarn remained glaring at the dog. The dog fox glared at Tarn and then walked off with brush held high back to Briar.

Tarn remained where he was until the dog fox was back with Briar. He licked his back leg, which was bleeding heavily. Eventually Briar and the dog fox walked off past the injured fox, the dog fox glared at Tarn as they did. They passed through the hedge up on to Ivinghoe Beacon. Later that night they mated.

Tarn lay shivering where he had fallen for the remainder of the night, licking his leg. Eventually the bleeding stopped but he was in a lot of pain. He was weak, cold and hungry. As night drifted into day Tarn moved from where he lay, by crawling to the sanctuary of a hedge. He lay there all that day and the following night licking his leg occasionally as he drifted in and out of consciousness. The leg was becoming infected from the deep puncture wounds inflicted by the dog fox.

The following morning, the weak winter sun rose above the hill behind Tarn, the sunlight cascaded through the hedge in long shafts, falling onto the weak and pain-ridden form. A mouse ran past him but he took little notice. He crawled out from under the hedge, the bright sunlight dazzling him momentarily. He limped across the field on three legs as he had little movement in his injured leg. He eventually reached the roadside hedge where he flopped down weak and exhausted. Traffic thundered past close to him.

That night he crawled to the edge of the road. Vehicles raced past, their thundering engines and dazzling lights terrifying the weak animal. He waited until he could not hear or see any danger and limped up onto the tarmac. Almost immediately the lights of a lorry came around the corner and bore down on him. Tarn looked at the lorry; he was dazzled by the lights and froze. Suddenly there was a loud blast from the lorry, Tarn attempted to leap clear but collapsed under his injured leg as the front wheels passed over him. Tarn was plunged into a loud and terrifying darkness as the lorry passed over him. As the rear wheels cleared him, the slipstream caught him and he rolled over and over until eventually he got to his feet and dashed as best he could on three legs to the safety of the hedge on the opposite side. The terrified fox passed through the hedge and out into the field beyond which he crossed. He looked a very dishevelled sight; his coat was matted with mud and blood. A freshly dug molehill on the other side of the field near a hedge provided him with a few worms before he entered the hedge and collapsed on to the ground, weak with pain and hunger. A penetrating frost only added to his misery.

He lay in the hedge all night, slipping in and out of consciousness as infection set into his injured leg. Before sunrise the following morning Tarn moved out from under the hedge and with his now paralysed leg held up, any movement of it sending shooting pain through his body. He moved off across the frozen ground, progress was very slow as he headed back to his own familiar territory. He was growing weaker and weaker as the infection took over his body, but instinct drove him on. He was having difficulty in focusing on features ahead of him as the infection affected his sight. Through sheer determination, by nightfall the weak, exhausted fox crawled in under the familiar hawthorn bush by the swing bridge on the canal at Beaconview. He tried to lick his injured leg but the pain was too much. The thigh muscle was swollen and badly infected.

Another penetrating frost did little to help the hapless creature curled up tight under the dense bush. The following morning the fox was totally disorientated, the infection had spread and a fever had set in. He was unable to focus; his world was spinning ahead of him. He crawled out on all fours into the sunlight and dragged himself down to the edge of the canal where the cattle had trodden down the bank. He lapped some water, ripples extending out across the mirror smooth surface. As he crawled back under the bush a magpie swooped down to mob him, but Tarn was unaware of the arrogant marauder who soon gave up his challenge.

For the next two days Tarn did not stir. He drifted in and out of consciousness as the infection took over his entire body. He was unaware of any danger that may have presented itself as he lay curled up. The sharp frosts and cold, clear, still, sunny days continued. Animals came and went as he lay there. An inquisitive stoat circled around Tarn before passing on its way. A hare that had been startled in the field took shelter under the bush and was further startled by the presence of the fox, and ran off.

On the third day Tarn was still unconscious. Rex had wandered on to the towpath on the opposite bank. He began to trot along the path in Tarn's direction, when the dog disturbed a water vole, which leapt into the water and began to swim under water, across the bank towards Tarn leaving a long line of bubbles. The vole suddenly surfaced in the middle of the canal. Rex gave out a loud and excited bark, which shattered the peace of the morning.

In an instant Tarn regained consciousness and was alert to the danger on the opposite bank. Rex was barking so excitedly that his front feet were leaving the ground.

Tarn shook his head and his vision cleared. He could see the labrador on the opposite bank. Tarn looked around and up into the bush. He had survived the infection and fever but was still very weak and was not in a fit state for a confrontation with Rex. As Tarn watched Rex, the vole disappeared into the undergrowth that overhung the canal. Rex continued barking. Tom Wright came up onto the towpath through the gate and shouted a command at Rex, which he ignored. Tom began to walk along the path, shouting at the dog, as Tarn watched from under the bush. Eventually Rex went quiet and followed Tom with his ears and tail down. They passed through the gate and out of sight of the fox.

Tarn remained under the bush until the following night when he emerged, still unable to walk on his injured leg. He was in a dishevelled state with his normal rusty red coat covered in matted mud and blood. He made his way towards the Iron Bridge but as he reached the embankment fence by the bridge a coal-laden narrow boat passed under the bridge, only a few feet from the fox. The scruffy man with a thick black jacket, black cap and a cigarette hanging out of the side of his mouth was staring ahead at the lock gates beyond the swing bridge. Tarn kept perfectly still as the danger passed.

Eventually Tarn limped along the embankment fence below the earth, away from the canal, as a train thundered past spewing its dense smoke over Tarn. As his nostrils cleared of the acrid smell, another scent reached him that spurred him on. His progress was very slow and difficult on three legs, but eventually he reached the source of the scent. It was a freshly killed rabbit in a 'Gin Trap'. Tarn made short work of this desperately needed meal.

He passed under the fence up onto the embankment; the slope was difficult for him to negotiate on three legs but he eventually reached the safety of the earth. He tried to clean himself up by licking off the mud and blood. His leg was still very painful. The next few days were difficult for Tarn. He only strayed a short distance from the earth, feeding on worms and beetles. A dead pheasant on the railway line was devoured where he found it.

The long road to recovery was slow and painful and was not helped by nature's intervention soon after Tarn had returned to the earth.

# Chapter Four
# THE FLOOD

As nature was about to burst forth with all its spring beauty, the elements were about to deal Tarn a savage blow.

A mild southwesterly wind brought rain one evening while Tarn was scavenging for food on his injured leg; he remained close to the earth. The rain grew heavier and heavier on the strengthening breeze. Tarn returned to the safety of the dry earth. The rain continued, unyielding in its ferocity. Trickles of rainwater were running down the embankment in tiny streams. In the morning Tarn was forced to leave the earth as water began to run in. As he ventured out the intensity of the rain on his face startled him and he fell back on his injured leg. He gave out a weak yelp, which was lost in the noise of the wind and rain.

He limped away still unable to put any weight on his leg. The rain soon drenched his muddy, blood-soaked coat. He limped down the embankment to the canal; the water was up to the very top. He climbed up onto a narrow concrete ledge, which extended under the iron bridge, on the opposite side of the canal to the towpath. A strong breeze was blowing under the bridge. He sat and licked his leg. A train thundered past overhead, the noise echoed under the bridge. He curled up and slept. A water vole swam across the canal from the towpath and emerged close to the resting fox. On sensing his presence it leapt back into the water and swam back under water.

He lay there for the remainder of the day but as dusk fell and he tried to leave the shelf, the scene that greeted, startled and confused him. The canal had burst its banks at the end of the shelf and water was cascading out in a torrent. His exit was effectively blocked. He crept along to the other end of the shelf on the other side of the bridge only to find everything the same here. He returned to the spot where he had slept and curled up. He was cold, wet and hungry and in a lot of pain from his leg. The wind and rain continued.

When Tarn woke halfway through the following day, the landscape that he was familiar with had changed. The fields that extended away from the base of the embankment were transformed into lakes as far as he could see. The orchard at Beaconview was under water, which was lapping at the floors of the huts in amongst the bare trees. Even the Nissen hut was flooded; Tom Wright had moved the chickens. Tarn was still trapped by the floodwater. He was frightened and growing weaker. There was no escape. The rain had now continued for four days and the wind whistling under the bridge had grown colder and was weakening the fox even more.

A further night under the bridge left Tarn shivering with cold, weak and hungry. As dawn rose the rain had eased a little and the torrent at the end of the ledge was reduced to a stream. Tarn ventured down off the shelf into the cold water. He waded belly deep through the muddy water to the foot of the embankment. He scrambled through the wooden fence and up onto the slope, still on three legs. A train thundered by as he limped along.

He sat down and licked his leg and as he did so the sun suddenly appeared from behind the slate grey blanket of a rain cloud. The rain continued and a huge rainbow appeared to partially encircle the orchard and house at Beaconview. The raindrops falling close to Tarn glistened in the brilliant sunlight. The rain suddenly stopped falling on him as it was blown away on the strong breeze. The rainbow faded and was gone as quickly as it had appeared. The black mass of cloud slowly moved away.

The landscape below Tarn was quite spectacular. The familiar fields were one big lake. The hawthorn bush that had offered Tarn shelter in the past stood stark and alone in the water. The henhouses in the orchard were casting dark shadows on the surface of the water. The brilliant blue sky reflected and shimmered on the surface of the water in the fields below Tarn, as the wind ruffled the surface.

Tarn shook himself and limped along the embankment. He reached the bramble where his earth was but the roof had partially collapsed due to the rain and he was too weak to clear it. He limped on and caught and ate an unwary beetle and a dead mouse. He rested up for the remainder of the day in the sun. As night fell a full moon rose in the sky. A few silver-white clouds scudded across the dark sky, reflected on the surface of the floodwater. The gentle breeze rippled the surface creating patterns. The quiet of the night was only broken by the hoot of a tawny owl in the Beaconview orchard. A train went by, its smoke silver in the moonlight, swirling around on the breeze. Tarn left the spot where he had rested and limped away in search of food still unable to walk on his leg, but some painful movement was returning slowly. He caught a few beetles and worms; the redwing and fieldfare had left no berries.

For the next few days he made do with morsels but as the floodwaters slowly receded an unexpected food supply presented itself to Tarn. As the floodwater became shallower, frantic activity began as fish that had been swept out of the canal on the flood torrent had become trapped. Herons from all around the district had descended on this food bonanza and Tarn limped down off the embankment. He had not eaten fish before but was soon feeding well. He would sleep on the embankment by day and feed by night.

With such a food supply his strength soon returned as he was forced to wander further and further in search of fish. He even ventured into the orchard at Beaconview. As he picked his way through the shallow water that was slower to go than that in the fields, he didn't notice the pond as its features were lost in the flood. As Tarn wandered he suddenly sank into the deep water of the pond and had to swim to safety. He shook himself; his coat was now clean of the blood and mud that had matted it for so long.

Eventually the floodwaters disappeared along with the last of the fish. His strength was back and he had put on weight. He was able to walk on his injured leg but it was still painful and he had a distinct limp.

Tarn had narrowly survived the fight with the dog fox and the flood, and some lessons for life had been learnt. The following summer was also to test Tarn's survival skills.

# Chapter Five
# THE LONG, HOT SUMMER

As the winter slowly gave way to spring, birds sang in excitement, insects buzzed everywhere and there was a stirring in the countryside. When the first cowslips and coltsfoot appeared on flower bringing a splash of yellow on the embankment, Briar gave birth to three cubs in her earth at the base of Ivinghoe Beacon. The blackthorn thickets along the slopes turned white with blossom, taking on the appearance of snow-laden bushes.

As the days lengthened and the sun's strength increased the first blossoms appeared in the Beaconview orchard. Hares were 'boxing' in the fields and were behaving very strangely. Groups of three or four were following each other around the fields until two would suddenly stop face each other and leap up on their rear legs 'boxing' at each other, with fur flying from the opponent, eventually ending with one or both leaping into the air and twisting their bodies at the same time. With his pronounced limp Tarn tried to stalk them when they drew closer to him but their speed and agility outclassed him every time and he gave up. He had taken to hunting during the day as well as at night; his leg was reducing his hunting skills.

The first litters of rabbits were being born and the water voles were raising families in their holes in the canal banks. The fieldfares and redwings that had feasted on the hedgerow larder through the winter were leaving for their breeding grounds further north. Huge flocks were 'chucking' as they passed high over Tarn. As these birds were leaving the first summer visitors were arriving. Chiffchaffs were calling from the trees in the orchard and in the oak tree by the lock gates. Soon afterwards the first beautiful transcending call of the willow warbler could be heard from the bushes and trees all around; spring had finally arrived.

Despite his injured leg, Tarn was listless, resting very little day or night. He was spending a lot of time at the old straw rick where the hunting was good and required little effort. Slowly the strength returned to his leg but a limp remained. He rested up amongst the rotting bales, often laying in the sunlight. Narrow boats chugged past on the canal nearby but he took little notice.

One evening after catching a rat, he passed through the hedge onto the towpath just after a narrow boat had gone by. He walked off in the opposite direction towards

Beaconview Lock. As he passed the gate leading to Seabrook Cottage, he could hear Rex barking excitedly in the orchard. He had chased a cat up into one of the big apple trees, and was leaping around on his hind legs barking at the cat who was glowering down at him, spitting hatred at him with an arched back.

Tarn continued on, over the swing bridge and up onto the embankment, as a train passed overhead, its smoke enveloping him momentarily.

The earth was partially caved in as he glanced at it. He passed over the railway line to the opposite slope and had just cleared the track when a train thundered past. Soon after it had gone Tarn picked up the scent of another fox from the direction in which the train had come. The scent was strong and Tarn's curiosity got the better of him and he walked off along the slope. He found a spot where the other fox had scent marked; Tarn sniffed at it for some time before moving on.

A little further on he found a second scent mark. He followed the scent further and further along the track past the football pitch at which point the scent trail led Tarn back over the railway track. Suddenly Tarn saw the motionless prone fox lying across the wooden sleepers on the edge of the track. Tarn approached cautiously sniffing the air with every step nearer. He leaned forward nervously and sniffed the fox's brush. There was no movement from the prone creature and Tarn sniffed at it long and hard. He recognised the scent. It was the dead body of the dog fox that had inflicted the injuries on him - the father of Briar's cubs. There was dried blood all around the dead fox's head, he had been killed by a passing train.

Tarn eventually left the dead fox and wandered back across the railway track, across the football pitch, over the road and up the track leading to Spinney Hill. A crescent moon was low in the evening sky as he entered the spinney. He was trying to surprise the grazing rabbits in amongst the sheep, but his injured leg was still hindering him, his dashes from the cover to the rabbits were slow and they were able to escape with ease. He suddenly froze and looked back at the cover from where a curious sound was coming. Almost immediately a familiar figure emerged from the undergrowth. It was the badger that as a cub he had played with on the hill. Tarn rushed over but the badger was now a large muscle bound male, and not very sociable. He grunted at the fox and shuffled off amongst the sheep. Tarn followed but was soon challenged by the ewes that, protecting their lambs, charged at him sending him scuttling in the cover. The badger disappeared into the dark, ignored by the sheep.

Tarn moved through the spinney and found the sett entrance. There was a large ball of dried grass to one side. Tarn passed down into the sett to investigate but had only travelled a short distance when he was met by a huge, very angry, sow that was suckling three cubs. Tarn hurriedly exited the sett in reverse, with the sow snapping at his muzzle. He ran out of the spinney and along the hedge running down the side of the hill. He passed two more badgers but they ignored him as they foraged for worms in the grass below the hedge.

The spring passed into summer with very little rain. The arrival of the swallows had brought warmer weather. The hedgerows were full of activity as the first broods began to fledge the nest. The abundance of rabbits and rodents made hunting easy after the trials of the winter. Briar's cubs were growing fast and were venturing out of the earth. Since the death of her mate she had managed to raise all three cubs on her own.

One evening Tarn was wandering towards Ivinghoe Beacon. He had killed a rat as he had leapt off the lock gate beam under the oak tree. He passed through the fields and hedges eventually reaching the busy main road. He chose his moment and dashed across the road, through the blackthorn thicket and into the field where he had fought the dog fox. The scent of Briar's earth was drifting down the slope of the hill on the gentle warm summer breeze.

Tarn followed the scent, through the grazing sheep onto the hill itself, where Briar's earth was situated on the edge of a small copse. Suddenly Tarn froze, for there ahead of him was a cub looking intently at him. The cub burst into a run towards him but checked himself abruptly when he realised that Tarn was not his mother. The little cub ran off with ears down and his tiny brush flailing in the breeze. He disappeared into the copse.

Tarn continued towards the earth entrance and the copse beyond, when he stopped abruptly a short distance from the earth. Three shy little faces appeared from the undergrowth, staring nervously at him. The boldest of the three crept gingerly forward, sniffing at Tarn as she drew nearer to him. Tarn stood still as the tiny vixen approached him with ears down and crouching bravely. As she drew nearer the remaining two came out of the undergrowth towards him. The vixen cub reached Tarn and sniffed his legs as he towered over her. He slowly lowered his head to smell her but she leapt back startled. She crept forward again and the other two reached him. All three now sniffed around his legs as he gently smelt them.

Suddenly Tarn leapt back in play and the three startled cubs froze momentarily before bursting into a scamper after him; the chase was on. Tarn led them into a tight circle in front of the earth, allowing them to get close to him before running off again with the three still in pursuit. He fell over playfully and the three leapt on to him with no hesitation. He sprang to his feet, the cubs dropping in all directions, ran off again in a circle with the cubs in hot pursuit. Around and around they went, the cubs were beginning to tire when a loud yap brought the playful group to an abrupt halt, the lead cub crashing into the back legs of Tarn.

Briar had returned with a dead rabbit and on seeing Tarn with her cubs, immediately dropped it and ran with teeth bared at Tarn, who fled across the field with a very angry and aggressive Briar snapping at his heels. The confused cubs leapt for the security of the earth. On and on the two foxes ran. Twice Briar had nipped Tarn's back legs as the chase continued through the blackthorn and across the road, a car narrowly missing the two foxes as it braked and swerved violently. Through the thicket on the opposite side and out into the field beyond, at which point Briar stopped running and simply watched as Tarn disappeared across the field. She returned across the road and back to the cubs that were deep down in the earth. On realising that Briar was no longer behind him Tarn slowed down and stopped, licked his back legs where she had nipped him and returned to the hawthorn bush near the swing bridge where he curled up and slept.

The hot, dry weather continued with searing daytime temperatures and hot nights. The ground became parched and cracked. The level of the canal had dropped significantly, exposing the grey mud along the edges, with only a narrow stream left in the middle. The narrow boats had long since been prevented from using the waterway due to the low water level. The mud had dried and cracked and had become firm enough for Tarn to walk on.

One hot evening as the full moon rose above Ivinghoe Beacon Tarn had ventured out along the towpath, past the orchard and the Seabrook gate. Just past the gate he jumped down from the path onto the mud and walked along sniffing the grass tussocks overhanging the canal. Suddenly a startled water vole leapt from a tussock through the air down onto the mud where it scampered towards the narrow channel of water, pursued by Tarn. The vole reached the water and immediately dived under the surface. As Tarn drew nearer to the water the mud under his feet was damp and sticky. His paws began to sink in the mud. Ignoring this he continued to approach the water as the vole surfaced on the other side and scampered across the mud towards the safety of the grass bank beyond. The sight of the vole spurred Tarn on as he began to sink lower and lower into the sticky blue-grey mud.

The vole made good its escape as Tarn began to struggle to free each leg from the mud. The more he struggled the deeper he sank until he was up to his chest and stuck fast. Although the terrified fox continued to struggle he was unable to lift any of his legs clear of the mud. Terrified and panting heavily he continued to struggle and sank deeper into the mud, he sank until it was up to his flanks. Exhausted, he laid his head on the surface of the mud, the edge of the water very close to where he was. A tawny owl perched in the oak tree by the lock looked down on the stricken fox. Through the night Tarn continued to struggle periodically but his efforts were draining his energy. As the dawn rose heralding another hot day, an exhausted Tarn rested his head on the mud.

The sun rose higher and higher in the clear blue sky, beating down on Tarn. His head and back were fully exposed to the full heat of the sun, which was unrelenting. Tarn was becoming weaker and weaker. He was slipping in and out of consciousness and was panting heavily.

The sound of a squeaking hinge of the Seabrook gate brought Tarn to his senses and he began to struggle again. The boy from the farm passed through the gate and up on to the path where his eyes fell immediately on the stricken fox ahead of him. The boy stepped down off the path onto the mud and began to approach Tarn. As he got nearer the baked mud turned to a wet and sticky surface, which stopped the boy in his tracks. He turned and slowly returned to the path and back through the gate, only to return a few moments later with a long plank of wood and a spade.

Back down on the mud the boy laid the plank down and slid it towards Tarn. He then carefully approached Tarn with the spade. Tarn was so exhausted that he lay terrified, hardly able to move. On reaching the fox the boy began to dig the mud away from around Tarn. Slowly a hole began to appear around Tarn, which slowly filled with water. As the hole grew deeper twice the boy nearly fell off the plank but he was determined to release the stricken animal. He cleared the mud from both sides of Tarn's flanks and then started at the rear end. Tarn lay motionless as the boy worked on, but as he sensed the mud being moved away from him he summoned up the energy for one last struggle. The boy was now working around his head and shoulders, talking quietly to Tarn as he did so.

Suddenly, with one huge effort Tarn struggled free and with over half of his body grey and caked in the slimy mud he leapt out of the muddy water, across the mud surface up onto the towpath, through the hedge and away. The boy watched with a smile as the fox disappeared. He pulled the plank back onto the path and returned it and the spade to the farm, careful not to tell his grandfather what he had done.

The hot sun and the struggling had taken its toll on Tarn; he was weak and hungry. He rested near the spring-fed pond, which was still full, until nightfall. The mud rapidly dried, matting his coat. A few beetles and a mouse were all he could catch. Later in the night he swam through the pond and the mud was washed from his coat. The clear water became grey and murky.

Tarn soon recovered from his ordeal as the long, hot, unforgiving summer continued.

# Chapter Six

# FIRE!

The long, hot summer continued to parch the ground and vegetation. Food was becoming scarce. Even the old straw rick that had always been dependable for rodents was barren, as more and more hunters competed for food. Despite all the problems that the summer had brought, Briar had successfully raised her three cubs, although one had been injured on the road when it was struck by a sidecar of a motorcycle and had left her with a permanent limp.

Early one morning Tarn was walking along the side of the railway line before the sun had risen. A mist hung over the fields below him as he passed the 'Duke of Wellington', a train thundered past blowing Tarn's fur and brush.

After the train had passed a familiar scent reached him. He crossed over the track and descended through the undergrowth on the embankment. The scent became stronger and stronger; it was a fox. Another train passed by, its smoke blocking the scent momentarily. A short way along the fence the source of the scent became apparent. The lifeless blood-stained body of a fox cub lay on the ground immediately below the fence. A wire ran from the dead animal's neck to the fence. The snare had cut deep into the fox's neck as it had struggled to release itself. Tarn sniffed at the cub that had come from a litter born on the other side of the airfield below Spinney Hill. Tarn stood looking at it for a while before heading back towards the canal.

Shortly after this encounter Tarn was hunting one evening on the fields between the lock and Ivinghoe Beacon. He was working through a line of tall willow trees when he caught the scent of a fox nearby. He walked on and came across a fox cub curled up in the field beyond the trees. The cub did not stir as he approached. As Tarn reached the cub, it looked up weakly, its eyes were full of mucus and it appeared to be very weak. A lot of its fur was missing; the mange had taken its toll. The cub returned to its sleep as a light breeze rustled the leaves in the trees towering above it. Tarn moved away and caught a mouse nearby. He brought it to the cub and placed it in front of its muzzle. He gently nuzzled the baby fox but it did not stir. Tarn remained with Briar's youngest for the remainder of the night but the following morning the cub was dead. Tarn eventually left the cub and returned to the lock gates where he crossed over. He went through the hedge into the meadow with the pond, its water shimmering in the sun. He lapped some water and slept in the crook of one of the leaning willows.

A few days after the cub's death, Tarn was in the wheat field below Spinney Hill, searching for an unsuspecting mouse or bird. High in the blue sky above him skylarks were singing, but all the time watching the fox far below them. Their young had fledged the nest but they were still wary of the predator. Tarn eventually emerged out onto a grassy strip between two fields and there in the middle was a young rabbit feeding. Tarn immediately dropped and began to stalk the unsuspecting rabbit. The skylarks had fallen silent, as a buzzard was soaring high above them, its eyes fixed on the same rabbit that Tarn was stalking. The big bird began to drop with folded wings towards the rabbit that was unaware of the unwanted attention despite sitting bolt upright twice to check that it was safe to continue eating the parched brown grass. Down and down the buzzard dropped as Tarn drew ever nearer his prey.

The buzzard was now on its final approach, swooping low and fast just above the wheat. Closer and closer it came. Suddenly Tarn spotted the buzzard as it appeared from the wheat and was about to lunge down on the rabbit. Tarn made a desperate leap for the rabbit but the buzzard did the same. In the confusion both Tarn and the buzzard were forced to take evasive action to avoid a collision. The buzzard flapped his wings furiously to gain height, scolding Tarn as it rose. A startled Tarn had disappeared into the wheat. The target of all this attention, the rabbit, had made its escape into the wheat.

None the worse for wear for his encounter with the buzzard, Tarn curled up in the wheat, which offered some shade from the searing heat of the sun. Four fields away to the west the penetrating sun was shining through a broken glass bottle and had started a small fire in the corner of a field of barley. The fire soon took hold and within a very short space of time, the flames were roaring through the crop on an ever-increasing front. A strengthening breeze was fanning the flames and whipping up the smoke into circling columns. Behind the flames the field was left black and smouldering in places, the breeze was whipping up the ash into swirls.

Hares, rabbits and deer were running ahead of the flames, which rapidly spread and fanned out creating a huge wall of fire and choking smoke. Tarn slept on, blissfully unaware of the approaching inferno. The burning ash had started secondary fires ahead of the main front, and this had the effect of sweeping around to the sides of where the fox was sleeping. Birds were flying away from the flames and it was the alarm call of a blackbird speeding over his head that brought Tarn to his senses. He sat up alert and wary. Far off he could hear a strange roar that was getting louder, and almost immediately the rank choking smoke reached his nostrils. As he ran off through the wheat away from the roar behind him, a hare raced past him followed by a rabbit. A crashing sound came towards him and a fallow doe raced past in the opposite direction. He could now hear the roar ahead of him so he swiftly changed direction.

On and on he ran the choking smoke all around. It seemed that in every direction that he ran, the fire was approaching. He was confused and terrified as he continually changed direction. Other animals were also running in every direction as the fire closed in on all fronts. A terrified fox cub ran past him hardly noticing him as it ran for its life. Tarn ran in a big circle but the flames had encircled him. The front of the fire was still roaring on towards the Cheddington Road and the humpbacked bridge. The circle of wheat where Tarn found himself was rapidly shrinking. He ran past the blackened dead body of a stoat and stopped immediately afterwards as there was a wall of flames ahead of him. He turned and ran and the flames singed his brush.

The main front of the fire had reached the tinder dry hedge and after a huge roar with flames leaping high into the sky, the hedge was reduced to a black smouldering skeleton. The grass verge beyond was alight; the fire had leapt the road and was roaring through the opposite hedge and into the field where the horse grazed, despite the efforts of a number of fireman, who had had to move their fire appliances rather quickly as the flames had raced towards the first hedge. Tom Wright had taken the horse back to Beaconview. The brown parched grass was soon alight, the flames racing across the field, towards the railway embankment.

The heat and the smoke were choking Tarn as he desperately searched for an escape from the terrifying inferno that was about to engulf him. As the last strip of wheat surrendered to the flames, Tarn saw a small gap in the flames and leapt high into the air through the gap. The flames singed his whiskers and his coat and brush were licked by the flames singeing his entire body. He landed in the ash beyond the flames, alive but blackened by the flames. He ran across the blackened desert, wisps of smoke rising in places. He passed the charred remains of the fox cub that he had been trapped with; he had died in his desperate attempt to escape. Tarn ran to the hedge in front of the spinney; a black skeleton was all that remained of the hedge and the spinney beyond. In the spinney he went straight to the badger sett and without any hesitation went straight down inside. A number of badgers were sheltering deep down inside and Tarn joined them, they took little notice of him, apart from one that sniffed the acrid burnt smell coming from his coat. The depth of the sett had saved the badgers' lives as the flames had roared through the spinney.

The fire raced on fanned by an increasing wind from the west. Black storm clouds were building beyond Spinney Hill. The fire had reached the embankment in several places and was rising towards the track as the clouds blotted out the sun. The sound of thunder could be heard in the distance. The fire had reached the track and burning flecks of ash had ignited the opposite bank when the first drop of rain fell; the first in a very long time.

Tarn spent some time grooming his coat trying to remove the singed coat, as the lightning flashed outside followed almost immediately by loud cracks of thunder and the rain came down in torrents. The sweet smell of the fresh rain after so long reached Tarn and the badgers. The heavy rain soon extinguished the devastating fire that had left the countryside black and desolate. The storm raged through the night, but moved on before dawn. When Tarn stirred out of the sett the air was fresh but full of the smell of ash. He moved off through the spinney, down the western side of the hill and onto the airfield. A tunnel provided shelter and an unwary rat, a meal. The storms continued for several days and the canal began to fill very slowly. The ash on the fields was washed into the deep wide cracks that were everywhere, leaving the fields flat and bare.

As the storms finally moved away completely, Tarn returned to the embankment above Beaconview. In the orchard during the days that followed there was a lot of activity as the apples, pears and plums were gathered in. Tarn looked on unobserved by day and hunted at night.

The long hot summer had finally come to an end. As the autumn progressed, stirrings in Tarn turned his thoughts again to finding a mate.

# *Chapter Seven*
# THE CAT

The longer nights and shorter days heralded the first 'cubbing' hunt. The master and the huntsmen gathered at The Swan before sunrise and after gathering in the hounds they set off along the road, past the playing fields bathed in smoke from a passing train. At the edge of the village they turned up a bridle path, which led to Spinney Hill. The hounds drew the hedge dividing the two fields but there was no fox scent. Eventually they were up on the towpath moving towards the iron bridge.

Suddenly the silence was broken by the yelp of a hound. Tarn was awake in a flash moving away from the earth and down off the embankment as a train thundered past. As the pack reached a point level with the earth but on the other side of the canal Scar gave out a blood-curdling howl and the huntsmen were aware that there was a fox in the vicinity on the opposite side.

The swing bridge beyond the iron bridge was across the canal and the pack, led by Scar was in full flight after Tarn who was running along the base of the embankment. Meanwhile, the huntsmen were close behind spread out across the field at full gallop. Tarn led the hunt in a full circle around the field. He reached the lock gate, leapt up on to the huge wooden beam and ran across the full lock. The pack followed but in their excitement crossing the gate three of the hounds fell in. The 'whipper in' dismounted and managed to pull the wet and bedraggled hounds out. They shook themselves next to him, showering him with water while he cursed.

Tarn had run through the hedge into the meadow near Seabrook; Scar and the remaining pack were close behind. They went around the pond and back onto the path; meanwhile the huntsmen had been forced to ride hard, then up to the Ivinghoe Road and across the bridge before going back along the towpath. Tarn was running straight at the approaching horses when he suddenly leapt back through the hedge taking Scar by surprise. He went through the rotten straw rick and across the field back to the pond. The pack lost his scent momentarily in the rick, but as soon as Scar found it the chase continued but not before Tarn had gained a good distance on the hounds.

He re-crossed the lock gate unseen by the bargie on the narrow boat that was dropping in the lock. The hounds had lost his scent again at the lock and were frantically quartering the ground as the huntsmen arrived. Tarn had made good his escape and disappeared behind the line of willows as the 'whipper in' gathered the hounds and the hunt moved off along the towpath past Seabrook Cottage towards the iron bridge and the Cheddington Road beyond.

Tarn rested for the remainder of the day under a hedge near the willows. At sunset he rose and had a good scratch.

He ate a passing beetle and then moved off back to the railway line. Having crossed the line he trotted across the field to the humpbacked bridge and the Duke of Wellington beyond. He sniffed around the car park and the wooden tables near the canal but found no discarded scraps.

He crossed over the bridge and down onto the towpath beyond. He trotted along the path towards Beaconview where he could hear Rex barking in the distance. Suddenly a scent reached him, which stopped him in his tracks. Briar was in the field beyond the iron bridge on the other side of the canal. Tarn broke into a run; there was a skip in his step. The swing bridge was not across so he ran at full speed to the lock where he crossed into the field.

Tarn ran back towards the railway line. Briar was hunting along the base of the embankment when Tarn reached her. He gave out a soft yelp in excitement as Briar ran off, checking behind to see if Tarn was following - he was. In and out of the rather bemused cows the pair ran. One cow ran at Briar with its tail held high in the air but the vixen took little notice. Tarn leapt at Briar a few times but she sidestepped him each time. Closer and closer to the canal they ran until Briar suddenly stopped in her tracks, startling Tarn. She then chased Tarn in and out of the cows. Short bursts at high speed then twisting and turning abruptly. The game continued for some time.

On reaching the edge of the canal with Tarn in close pursuit, Briar halted abruptly; Tarn unable to stop leapt over her and sailed through the air before crashing into the cool canal. He sank deep into the water and emerged moments later coughing and spluttering. He swam to the side and pulled himself out dripping everywhere then shook himself hard, water cascading from him.

He looked around for Briar but she was gone. He followed her scent to the iron bridge and along the concrete shelf where he had been trapped during the flood. Coming out on the other side of the bridge he lost her scent. Once again she had eluded him.

For the next few days Tarn was restless after his encounter with Briar. He ate very little during the lengthening nights, spending most of his time searching for Briar. Finally one night he was in the fields below Ivinghoe Beacon when the peace of the night was pierced by a screech that brought Tarn to a stop. On top of the hill way above him, Briar was calling. Tarn ran across the main road and the fields, past Briar's earth and on up the steep slope of the hill. Briar gave out another screech, which spurred Tarn on even quicker.

He reached the top and ran past the concrete plinth trig point, similar to the one on Spinney Hill; Briar had dropped down the other side. She called a third time and Tarn yelped excitedly. He ran down the hill, and there she was ahead of him standing on a tussock on the steep slope.

On seeing him she ran off and the chase was on again. In and out of the grazing sheep they ran, up to the trig point and down the other side before running across the road, narrowly missing a lorry that braked hard when the driver saw the pair. On and on they ran, Briar occasionally looking over her shoulder to check that Tarn was still behind her.

He was determined not to lose her again. The full moon was rising in the night sky and daylight was almost gone as the pair reached the banks of the canal, both panting heavily after their long chase.

They stopped and both leaned down to the water for a drink. Briar came up to Tarn and rubbed her head against his neck. Tarn leapt back a little startled, and a playful chase began. The vixen ran to the lock gate where she jumped up on to the beam and as Tarn went to follow he yapped loudly as they met. On the tow path the other side they slowly encircled each other sniffing each other's coats as a tawny owl flew out of the oak tree and glared at them as it flew low over the foxes and the hedge beyond.

As the foxes continued playing, they were unaware of a pair of eyes watching them from the bottom of the hedge behind the path nearby. Unnoticed by the foxes, a huge black & white tomcat was crouched under the hedge watching the foxes with his bright green eyes, which were filled with hatred. The very tip of his tail was flicking furiously from side to side. His coat was thick and shiny. His left ear was broken and folded over from a previous fight.

The foxes played without a care in the world, leaping up with paws on each others shoulders, with mouths open, each trying to reach higher than the other. Both were yapping loudly and were slowly moving towards the hidden cat who was becoming angrier and angrier. Suddenly the cat leapt out from under the hedge on to the path, and stood spitting and hissing at the pair whose play was brought to an abrupt halt. They stood staring at the huge cat. The cat's ears were down and his body rigid. Tarn leapt forward, challenging the cat, but was startled as the cat lunged forward swiping at him with his paws, just missing Tarn's face. Tarn leapt back in surprise and the cat, seizing the advantage, pressed home its attack and struck out again at Tarn catching him on his rear flank, the needle sharp claws sinking into his flesh.

With a loud yelp he ran off with the cat chasing him. Briar leapt up on to the lock gate and watched the two disappear into the night. Tarn was at full stretch; for its size the huge cat had surprising agility and was gaining on the fleeing fox. They ran past Seabrook Cottage and the swing bridge, under the iron bridge, through the hedge on the other side and into the field where the horse was standing. He watched as they passed by him. Tarn ran back to the path and sensing that the cat was now close, he was forced to take a desperate measure. With one flying leap he took off and crashed down into the water and swam to the opposite bank. The cat did not follow; he stood and watched as the fox reached the other side and clamber out. Tarn shook himself after checking that the cat wasn't behind him and ran off to the embankment before crossing the railway track and returning to the earth. His flank had stopped bleeding but it remained sore for a few days. His mind was set on finding Briar again.

# Chapter Eight
# BADGER TO THE RESCUE

The search for Briar began in earnest again as his flank recovered but try as he might he could not find her. Tarn returned to the earth one cold, misty, damp morning after another unsuccessful night's searching. As he entered the earth a narrow boat passed under the iron bridge and a train thundered past overhead. He rested deep down in the dark dry earth.

In Cheddington the hunt were gathering in the car park of The Swan. After the cubbing hunts this was the first full hunt of the season in this area. The 'field' was large with nearly thirty horses assembled. A lot of the villagers had assembled to see the spectacle. As the 'whipper in' rode up through the High Street with the hounds, the mist began to clear and a hazy sun was appearing. Trays of drinks were brought out of the pub for the riders who were all busy talking about the prospects for the day's hunting.

Eventually the hunt master Colonel Foster-Smythe led the hunt away from the car park, following the pack to the edge of the village where they turned off the road onto the bridle path and Spinney Hill beyond. The 'whipper in' took the hounds along the hedge below the hill and down the hedge back to the road, at which point he blew his horn to gather the hounds in. Tarn woke with a start as the sound of the distant horn reached his ears. He sat up and moved out of the earth and up on to the railway track, scenting the air and listening intently as the low sun spread his shadow across the tracks. He moved off along the track towards the village. He disappeared into the undergrowth as a train thundered past, only to move back up on to the track once it was safe.

The hunt had crossed the road and was in a field next to the lane leading to Beaconview. It was drawing closer and closer to Tarn who was still moving along the track, which disappeared into the distance ahead of him. A buzzard was drifting in circles in the blue sky way above him. Tarn crossed the track and descended the embankment then disappeared in the dead undergrowth. The hunt was now behind him and some way off, but heading in his direction.

Suddenly Scar, at the head of the pack, gave out a cry that galvanised the entire pack and the field behind; Tarn's scent had reached him. The chase was on. Tarn heard Scar and ran down the embankment and across the grass field beyond. After crossing the Cheddington Road, he ran through the hedge and across the field towards Spinney Hill. The pack was in full chase strung out behind him with Scar at the lead. One huntsman had been detailed to ride along the hedge towards the hill to try and head Tarn off but Tarn was too quick.

Onto the hill he ran, the grass damp under his pads. He went over the top and past the trig point then down through the scrub on the other side before going onto the airfield; the hounds were beginning to gain on him. A startled hare ran off immediately in front of him. On and on he ran moving in a huge arc around the field, through willow scrub and eventually back towards the hill. As he approached, a huntsman was sitting at the base of the hill and as Tarn approached him he stood in his saddle shouting and calling "Charlie's away" and frantically waving his hat. Tarn ignored him and ran back onto the hill, and past the trig point again. On the other side another huntsman was sitting near the hedge at the base of the hill and on spotting Tarn began calling "Charlie's away". Tarn turned and ran into the spinney. The lead hounds were now close behind and running flat out. Scar was almost on Tarn's brush. The hounds were crashing through the undergrowth behind him. The entrance of the sett appeared ahead of him and without a break in his step he bolted into the darkness. Down and down he went until the tunnel opened out onto a large chamber and there sitting quietly at the back were two badgers.

The hounds were all gathered around the entrance to the sett, Scar continually put his head down the hole but he was too big to fit down the tunnel. The field had gathered on the hill and two men had arrived in a Land Rover. They parked it at the base of the hill and walked to the spinney with a terrier on a rope lead. The 'whipper in' blew his horn and took the hounds away from the sett as the 'terrier men' arrived. Tarn could hear the human voices at the end of the tunnel and pressed himself against the dirt wall. The badgers had not moved but simply sat quietly in the dried dead grass bedding.

The terrier was slipped from its lead and immediately entered the sett and approached the fox down the tunnel; its scent reached Tarn. The rough haired brown Jack Russell suddenly appeared in the chamber and immediately the two badgers darted forward and attacked the startled terrier, which yelped loudly as the badger's teeth ripped his mouth. As he moved back into the tunnel a little dazed, one of the badgers seized the advantage and pressed home the attack; there was only room for one badger in the tunnel. The terrier moved back a little further and realising that only one badger was able to follow her she lunged forward again at the sow.

The sow was ready and as the little dog opened her mouth the badger grabbed the top jaw of the terrier, who yelped in pain as the sharp teeth sank into her muzzle. The dog tried to spring back but was held fast by the powerful jaws of the badger. The terrier struggled violently, desperately trying to get away from the sow who began reversing back down the dark tunnel towards the chamber where Tarn was hiding behind the boar. The terrier desperately tried to get a purchase on the clay/chalk floor but she was no match for the strength of the sow. The men were calling to the little dog from the entrance to the sett, realising that she was in mortal danger.

Eventually the dog and badger reached the chamber and as the hapless terrier was dragged into the open space the boar lunged forward and grabbed her by her left flank; the dog gave out a terrified yelp. The sow momentarily released her iron grip on the terrier's jaw and the dog leapt backwards into the tunnel, bleeding heavily from her flank and jaw.

The dog backed up the tunnel as fast as she could but the sow followed and bit the her twice more in the ear and flank, before returning to the chamber. The sight that greeted the men when their dog reappeared at the entrance to the sett shocked them both. She was covered in dry dirt and blood. Her face was just a mass of blood, and bright red blood was seeping from the deep wound on her left flank inflicted by the boar in the chamber. Skin was hanging off her mouth and she could hardly open her left eye; she was a pathetic sight. She was picked up by one of the men and gently placed in her box in the back of the Land Rover.

The master and the huntsmen were shocked by the extent of her injuries, and were surprised that she was in fact still alive. The hunt eventually rode off behind the hounds, down the hill towards the canal; the huntsmen were talking amongst themselves about the state of the terrier, wondering if she would survive.

Tarn remained in the sett with the badgers for the remainder of the day and, in the early evening, cautiously emerged from the dark tunnel where the smell of the terrier's blood was still strong, as pools of it lay on the floor of the tunnel. He wandered off down the hill to the road, through the hedge on the other side and across the field where the old ginger Suffolk Punch was standing in the corner. He went up onto the railway embankment as a train thundered past then over the tracks as the rear of the train rapidly disappeared into the distance. He caught an unwary mouse just off the track and returned to the safety of the earth.

The badgers soon recovered from their ordeal, but the terrier took a long time to recover. Tarn began his search for Briar again not knowing that she was also looking for him.

# Chapter Nine
# THE FAMILY

The two foxes met up again under the tall oak tree by the lock gates one evening. A full moon was high in the sky as they greeted each other with flattened ears and brushes lowered and swept to one side.

A noisy game of 'tag' then followed around the broad tree trunk and out across the field to the willows, where they chased each other in an out of the trees and back, the pursuer becoming the pursued. The two foxes were oblivious to the world around them as the games reached a crescendo of noise, which woke Rex at Beaconview. He started barking but a loud shout from Tom Wright quietened him down. The brilliant moon played with their shadows on the frosty ground as the games continued and ultimately they mated twice. As dawn rose, the foxes rested under the trees, curled up close to each other. The weak winter sun rose a little and shone down through the bare trees onto the resting pair.

They remained there for the rest of the day, but as night fell a cold freezing fog enveloped the countryside and the foxes. They went off hunting and Tarn caught an unwary rabbit, which he shared with Briar. They crossed the field and the swing bridge beyond then went along the towpath and under the iron bridge before running up the embankment on the other side. A train thundered past; the lights of the carriages flickered on the foxes, its smoke lost in the swirling fog in the slipstream of the last carriage - the guard's wagon. They played outside the earth as the courtship continued, standing on hind legs with their front legs on each other's shoulders, they wrestled with mouths opened and played on and on through the night, mating twice more.

They remained together hunting and playing at night and sleeping during the cold days. The longest night passed and soon after it was the time of the strange lights in the village, festooned all over the large conifer outside The Swan pub and in the windows of the houses and over small trees in their gardens. One evening the two foxes were hunting and had found themselves on the edge of the village, moving stealthily through the front gardens of the houses on the opposite side of the road to the pub. There was music coming from the car park of the pub and a large group of people were standing around the tree with the strange lights on, singing. A brazier was burning nearby with flames leaping from the top and through the holes in the side, as the wood crackled within. The foxes sneaked away after watching the people with some curiosity. Briar caught a mouse and Tarn found a dead pheasant on the road near the railway station. They returned to the earth along the railway line, avoiding the centre of the village.

Two days later the hunt met again at The Swan Hotel. It was a bright sunny crisp morning, the hunt master Colonel Foster-Smythe looked resplendent on his huge bay horse as the low sun fell on his red coat and polished black boots with their brown tops. The field all stood around on their horses, making polite conversation and sipping their sloe gin. The 'whipper in' led the hounds up the High Street, through the village with Scar at the lead, to the front car park at the hotel and joined the rest of the field. A short while later the Master led the way out of the car park and out of the village in the general direction of the canal. As he left the last house he turned through a field gateway and off towards Spinney Hill, where Tarn had been the previous night.

The two foxes were curled up deep in the warm, dry earth, unaware of the hunt way off across the fields on the other side of the railway track. Tarn had left a good scent trail and it was not long before Scar was on it. The hounds were singing with excitement as they ran across the field towards the towpath. Through the hedge they dashed; the master and the field had doubled back and were on the road, galloping towards the humpbacked bridge, under which the hounds had already passed when the field reached it. They rode single file down from the road and onto the path as the 'whipper in', who was following the hounds, disappeared around a bend just prior to the iron bridge. The field went into full gallop in single file along the narrow path with a high hedge on their left. Tarn had heard the approaching hounds and had left the safety of the earth, leaving Briar there. He trotted down the embankment to the field below and off in the general direction of Ivinghoe Beacon. The swing bridge was across the canal and the hounds used it to cross the icy water. They lost the scent momentarily but Scar soon found it. Singing loudly the pack ran towards the embankment where they picked up Tarn's fresh scent; the chase was on again. Briar sat tensely with her ears forward. At the back of the earth she could hear that the hounds were close but as she sat the hounds' calls died away as they followed the trail that Tarn had laid.

Tarn was now at full stretch but was gaining distance on Scar who was ahead of the pack. Tarn led the hunt in a huge semi-circle through three fields before eventually heading back to the canal. He reached the swing bridge and ran across then turned right towards Seabrook Cottage and the lock gates beyond. Just after passing the cottage he dived through the hedge as Scar was just passing over the swing bridge. Scar and the pack ran along the towpath but the field, on realising where Tarn was headed, raced back along the towpath to the hump-backed bridge. They ran up onto the road and in full gallop back down the road towards Cheddington and off right into the lane leading to Beaconview and the other farms, in an attempt to head Tarn off.

Tarn ran past the pond and into the farm of Stan Kingham. Scar and the pack were beginning to gain ground on Tarn as he weaved in and out of the high stacks of straw bales, which were dotted all over the place. He came racing around the corner of a barn and found himself in the main yard of the farm. Feeding quietly in the morning sunlight were a flock of about forty plump chickens and Stan Kingham had just put a load of wheat mash out for them. Without hesitation Tarn ran straight through the middle of them, sending most of them squawking and flapping in panic in all directions. As Tarn cleared the yard and disappeared, Scar and the pack rounded the corner as the startled chickens were still running in all directions at the sight of the fox. The hounds, many of which were new, became totally confused and excited at the sight of these chickens and they immediately began chasing the chickens in all directions. The 'whipper in' arrived and desperately tried to bring the pack under control by blowing his horn and cracking his whip, both of which had little effect. The only hound that came to his side was Scar. The remainder of the pack were eventually brought under control as the master arrived.

Stan Kingham came to the front door of his house to see what the commotion was. The sight that greeted him sent him into a rage; at least six chickens lay dead in the yard. He shouted at the 'whipper in' and the master, so loudly that Tarn heard it as he made good his escape across the railway track, leaving the devastation behind him. He crossed the field and the road and trotted up on to Spinney Hill. The hunt master apologised for the carnage caused by the hounds that were gathered around the 'whipper in' in disgrace. Suitable financial restitution was offered and accepted. The hunt did not ride at Cheddington for the remainder of that hunting season. As night fell Tarn returned to the earth with a rabbit for Briar.

A few weeks later the pair found themselves in danger again, this time from poachers. The foxes had returned to the earth after an unsuccessful night's hunting; Briar was now heavy in cub and Tarn was hunting for her. A cold, damp mist shrouded the embankment and the countryside beyond. As the foxes slept three men had parked their car in the gateway of the field where the horse was and had climbed up onto the embankment to get some rabbits. They crossed the railway line and started walking along the embankment towards the earth.

They were scruffy looking individuals: unshaven, shabby coats tied around the waist with baling twine, caps perched on the side of their heads. Each man was carrying a box containing a ferret and some nets. They stopped a number of times and placed the nets over some of the rabbit holes and the ferret was put down to flush out the rabbits. The terrified rabbits would race out of the holes, into the nets and then the men would grab them. A train thundered past and the men crouched down, unseen by the train driver who was busy stoking the boiler, his mate was looking out of the engine on the other side from the poachers.

As the sound of the train disappeared into the distance, the squeal of a rabbit caught in one of the poachers' nets brought Tarn to his feet his ears straining to hear the rabbit. A shout from one of the men as he tried to catch his ferret, reached Tarn who immediately bolted into the depths of the earth where Briar had awoken and was crouched in the chamber at the end of the tunnel. They sat side-by-side listening.

The poachers passed over the bridge, over the lane by walking along the tracks, and went back down onto the embankment to search for a few more rabbit holes with their ferrets as they approached the iron bridge over the canal. On reaching the second bridge they went back up onto the track, passed over the canal and back down onto the embankment before going towards the earth where the two foxes sat anxiously listening to the approaching danger.

Closer and closer the voices grew; there were no rabbit holes near the earth. One of the men suddenly spotted the entrance to the earth amongst the bare bramble, and approached. The other two stood further up the embankment, above the earth. On realising that it was not a rabbit warren, he spoke to the other two. He then reached into the pocket of his coat and brought out a hand-made brass wire snare with a wooden peg attached. He climbed through the bramble to the earth's entrance, pushed the peg into the ground, opened the snare up into a circle and fixed it over the entrance. Satisfied that it was set, he moved out of the bramble and joined the other two, talking excitedly. A fox pelt would be a bonus for them, fetching good money within the fur trade.

The men moved on a little further then crossed over the track and began to walk back along the opposite embankment towards the village, where they had parked their car near the playing fields. They planned to check the snare the following day.

They caught several more rabbits on the way back, but on reaching their van they were met by the local policeman PC Bennett. He had been tipped off by Tom Wright at Beaconview that the poachers were on the embankment. All their catch was seized, and they eventually appeared before the local Justice of the Peace Colonel Foster –Smythe.

The fog persisted all day and the foxes remained in the safety of the earth until after dark when Tarn began to stir. He had a stretch and a scratch and sniffed at Briar who was still resting. He moved out of the chamber and along the tunnel towards the entrance. Suddenly the scent of human reached his nostrils and he froze. He remained perfectly still for a long time, but there was no sound of humans outside. He crept forward to the entrance and was about to pass into the snare, which would surely have killed him when he spotted the wire noose with his nose. He stopped and sniffed at the lethal wire trap, which was blocking his path. The rank scent of human and metal filled him with fear.

Fortunately the snare was not completely covering the entrance and Tarn found a gap on one side. After a lot more careful investigation, Tarn gingerly moved forward down the side of the snare and as he moved out the wire loop passed down his side. He cleared the snare and turned to look, Briar was following but was about to put her head into the snare. Tarn snapped a warning at her and she jumped back. He went back to the snare, which although had moved as he passed it, was still over the entrance. He began to investigate it from outside and soon located the wooden peg.

Gingerly he bit onto the peg and began to pull, but it did not give. He took a firmer grip and pulled harder and harder but still it wouldn't move until with one huge tug it suddenly came free sending Tarn rolling over and over backwards. When he got to his feet he noticed that the snare had dropped around his leg but it had not closed tight and he carefully stepped out of it. Carefully he picked the snare up by the soil-laden peg and carried it down to the bottom of the embankment where he dropped it. Briar gingerly left the earth and joined Tarn. She was now heavy with cub and only hunted with Tarn for a short while before returning to the earth. A dead hare on the road near the hump-backed bridge fed them both that night.

A few nights later as snow fell outside in a bitter easterly wind, Briar gave birth to three cubs, two dogs and a vixen; Tarn's first litter. He was rather curious at the three naked balls of flesh, which wriggled into Briar's side and began suckling, even before they were dry.

Tarn moved outside but the snow forced him back into the entrance and out of the bitter wind. The snow continued all night and the following morning. By nightfall of the second day both Briar and Tarn were hungry so Tarn moved off into the deep snow in search of food. The snow was deep in places but luck was on his side; he found a partially covered dead wood pigeon that had been struck by a train in the blizzard. Tarn carried it back to the earth, where Briar snatched it from him at the entrance and returned to the cubs.

This set the routine for the next few weeks. Tarn was hunting for both of them and was forced to hunt during the day as well as at night. Briar would not let him near the cubs and so he slept just within the entrance. Fortunately the cold spell only lasted three days and the thaw was rapid as a long mild spell came in. This encouraged the rabbits to begin breeding and baby rabbits became the staple diet of both foxes.

The yellow flowers of the coltsfoot were the first to appear in patches along the embankment. Snowdrops appeared under the hedge near the towpath gate to Seabrook Cottage. The first summer migrant, a chiffchaff, began to sing from the tall oak by the lock gate as winter left with a sting in its tail. Four very cold days followed with an icy blast from the north and a light dusting of snow. With Tarn providing food for Briar, the cubs rapidly grew. Their eyes opened and they began to move around the inner chamber of the earth under the ever-watchful eye of Briar.

The warmth of spring brought leaf cover on the bramble over the earth, concealing it from prying eyes. One morning after a successful night's hunting, Tarn was lying just outside the earth with shafts of sunlight cascading through the bramble onto him. His eyes were shut but his ears flickered, as they remained alert for any sounds of danger. Very quietly a little face appeared nervously at the entrance, its eyes blinking in the bright sunlight. Tarn looked up with an enquiring glance, as a second and third head appeared, Tarn looked on motionless as the three cubs blinked and sniffed the air, only to dart back down into the safety of the earth as a train thundered past overhead, the white smoke rolling down the bank and through the bramble.

As the weeks went by the cubs grew braver and were regularly out of the earth playing in the bramble, as Tarn had done as a cub so long ago. One warm summer day, Tarn was lying outside the earth with Briar by his side. The cubs were playing with his brush as he flicked it from side to side. He looked out across the countryside below him. Tom Wright was scything down the tall cow parsley in the orchard at Beaconview, whistling as he took big sweeps with the blade. Swallows were skimming the surface of the canal. A skylark was singing high in the clear blue sky above the earth. A whitethroat was scolding the cubs from a nearby blackthorn bush. A turtledove was purring from the tall oak tree near the lock gates. The air was full of the sounds of insects busily feeding. High in the sky swifts were flying effortlessly, feeding on the insects that ventured too high. A train passed above the earth and a narrow boat chugged along the canal.